THE
DEPTHS
OF **LOVE**

LOVE THY ENEMY

AN SFWG ANTHOLOGY

All stories in this collection are the creation of the author's imagination and are intended for entertainment purposes only. Any resemblance to person, places, events, etc. - living or dead - is purely coincidental, or used in a fictitious manner.

Published by:
Cloaked Press, LLC
PO Box 341
Suring, WI 54174
https://www.cloakedpress.com

Cover Design by:
Fantasy & Coffee Design
https://www.fantasyandcoffee.com/SPDesign/

With Stories From:

Matias Travieso-Diaz

David Dixon

Laura J. Campbell

Johnathon Heart

Jennifer Jeanne McArdle

Barend Nieuwstraten III

August Blaine Centauri

Fern KL Goodliffe

Andrei-Ion Ghircoiaş

Frank Sawielijew

J. L. Royce

TABLE OF CONTENTS

Gwarwyn Goes Fishing

by Matias Travieso-Diaz

Gwarwyn was a *bwbach*, a humanoid known outside Wales as a brownie. He dwarfed other creatures of his kind, and thanks to his keen senses of sight and hearing he could perform for his human hosts tasks not usually given to *bwbachs*, such as protecting domestic animals from wolves and other predators.

Early on Whitsuntide evening, Gwarwyn had gone fishing on the river Neath, taking advantage of the summer weather. The Neath ran a meandering course through southwestern Wales until it plunged into the Horseshoe Falls, not far from where Gwarwyn had positioned himself. He stayed on the bank, because although the river bed was gravelly and gave good purchase, the current in the stretch leading to the falls was swift and there was always a chance of slipping.

As he sat on the river bank, the evening sky darkened and threatening clouds rolled in from the west. Gwarwyn was unaware of the change in the weather, because his eyelids had turned heavier and sleep had overtaken him.

He looked up with a start. His keen hearing had detected, some distance away, the sound of cries. The sounds were approaching, so he moved back from the bank a little trying to get a view of whatever was causing the commotion.

Finally, the source of the disturbance became visible: a raft was heading down the river, coming in his direction. The cries were emitted by a human female that was clutching a seat on the center of the structure as it moved randomly, drawn here and there by the current.

Despite the darkness, it took only a glance for Gwarwyn to recognize Anwen – the daughter of Tudur ap Gruffydd, a wealthy landowner in the kingdom of Dyfed. Tudur was one of the humans for whom Gwarwyn worked, tending to his fields at night and protecting his lambs from predators.

Gwarwyn had sometimes spied on Anwen when events drew him abroad during daytime, like county fairs and religious festivities. She was always nicely dressed, always smiling. A couple of times they had run into each other in the manor house's kitchen, where every evening Gwarwyn was left on the hearth food (oatmeal cakes were his favorite), clothing items, and other presents, all intended to entice him into staying at the estate.

In each occasion they met, Anwen had averted her face with disgust and left without addressing him. Gwarwyn had greenish skin, was very hairy, and had a wrinkle-covered face, all of which made him unsettling or frightening to some humans.

Gwarwyn had secretly longed after Anwen. He often admired from afar the perfect oval of her face, the softness of her body. Yet, he knew she loathed him.

As the raft approached, Gwarwyn noticed that Anwen's auburn hair, which he had always itched to caress, was shooting in all directions, buffeted by the breeze. She was pale as if she had seen a ghost, and trembled as the raft made steady progress towards the falls.

Gwarwyn jumped into the river and, as he did so, a strong wind began to blow, gathering intensity until its blasts swept the countryside. The wind roiled the waters and impeded his progress as he swam towards the raft, which was rising and falling with loud splashes, its timbers lifted and tossed by the force of the storm. Gwarwyn's considerable strength served him well, as he was able to overcome the tumbling of the frenzied Neath as he approached the vessel.

At last, Gwarwyn seized the side of the raft, coming close to being brained by a sudden jolt of the structure. He clung to the slippery logs for dear life and, with a wrenching effort, pulled himself onboard. In the back of the raft, Anwen watched him in horror, her fear of the elements eclipsed by the sight of a creature in soaking rags that came tumbling towards her with obviously evil intent. She recognized Gwarwyn, and seeing him brought back the memories of their meetings and the multitude of folk tales she had heard about brownies' malevolence.

Gwarwyn reached her and extended a hairy hand, beckoning the girl to join him. "Come on, lady, let me carry you out to safety," he grumbled. Anwen did not move but rolled herself into a defensive ball as he approached. "No, go away, dirty *bwbach*, leave me alone!!" she cried, clutching desperately at her seat.

"Come on, please, there is no time to waste!!" Gwarwyn insisted, and reached out to seize her arm. She pushed him away and got up, lurching towards the side of the raft, intending to go in the river.

As Anwen readied to jump off, Gwarwyn thrust headfirst at her, trying to stop her from plunging to a certain death. She flung her arms out at him in a protective move. They collided and catapulted together into the water. The impact with the water drained at once all resistance from Anwen, who clung to Gwarwyn, gasping.

Gwarwyn looked at the girl and then at the raft, whose surface had almost disappeared from sight. There was a crushing sound: the raft had been propelled against a protruding rock and had splintered into a thousand pieces, disintegrating from bow to stern. Gwarwyn clutched Anwen's body closer to his and covered her body with his to protect against the flying wreckage.

The forward pull of the river as they approached the falls became stronger. Gwarwyn made out a disturbance in the waters ahead, a vortex into which the floating detritus was being drawn. He put his left arm around Anwen so that he could steer them both clear of the raft remnants that sailed past them in the current. He tried to push the floating objects away with his one free hand as the river thrust them against him. The ones he could not avoid hitting he met with his body to save the girl from injury.

The falls came into sight. Gwarwyn looked around anxiously, searching for a way out. The river banks were near but out of reach, for the current kept him, burdened by the girl's weight, from making headway towards the shore. There was nothing left to hold onto; even the wreckage from the raft had gone into the abyss. Gwarwyn stretched his legs as far down as he could, but failed to touch bottom.

The waters became white with froth, and broke into an irregular circular motion. Gwarwyn could tell from the mist rising about the surface that they were about to start gyrating and plunge down the falls to their deaths. The maelstrom was only twenty feet ahead. Then, he saw something that stuck out of the water from a pole at the shore to another in midstream -- a thick rope net strung just above the whirling surface of the river. Wreckage from the raft, tree limbs, roots and rocks were caught in the net's webbing, as well as countless dead fish.

Gwarwyn felt relief rise in his chest, to be squelched by the realization that they were likely to be impaled on a sharp piece of flotsam or a nail-covered board. He maneuvered with inhuman strength, further increased by desperation, to find a relatively empty corner of the net. He found one and allowed himself and the girl to be slammed into it.

The ropes that formed the netting gave a little so their impact against them was not too painful, but the strain of the rushing waters pushing around them towards the falls made Gwarwyn feel as is his flesh was being strained into a liquid mass that would be sucked in by the net and then released into the maelstrom.

With a supreme effort, Gwarwyn began to advance towards the shore along the netting, holding onto one of the tie lines. He had to let go of Anwen's body, who mercifully continued to cling onto him. Hand over hand, inch by inch, he made the excruciating trip along the rope, resisting the push of the stream that drew them towards the falls. Twice he faltered and almost let go; each time, Anwen's groans gave him renewed strength and saved them both from certain death. He continued on until at last his feet found the gravel at the river bottom. He half walked, half propelled himself and Anwen towards the river bank.

Before reaching the safety of the shore, they came upon a large moss-covered boulder by the water's edge. Gwarwyn laid Anwen down on the rock, prying her fingers loose, as she would not let go of him. With an exhausted sigh, he collapsed on the rock next to her. He could go no further.

They lay there for a very long time, recovering from the shock and the pain that throbbed through their bodies. At last, Gwarwyn turned over on his side and contemplated the girl. She was wearing a jerkin over a plain blouse, loose fitting brown trousers and leather boots – not unlike his own uniform. Her jerkin was torn and open, and her breasts heaved up and down

5

under her blouse with her irregular breathing. She was slowly regaining consciousness, shuddering from the cold.

Anwen's hair was matted and covered her eyes. Gwarwyn ran his hand over her forehead to straighten it out, and halfway through his gesture it became a gentle touch. Unable to control himself, he let his hand slide over her cheek and traced with his index the curve of her upper lip.

Anwen opened her eyes and looked vacantly into Gwarwyn's face, just above hers. "Are you hurt?" asked Gwarwyn in a soft voice, holding her chin in his hand.

Anwen then gave a start and came awake. She said nothing but put her arms around Gwarwyn's neck, as if seeking reassurance after their near-death experience. Gwarwyn pivoted on his free arm and let his body drop carefully beside Anwen's. They stared at each other without words, still prey to the terror they had just shared.

On a sudden uncontrollable impulse, Gwarwyn pressed his lips against the girl's in a stream of kisses, at first soft and then increasingly more passionate. Anwen did not resist but responded in kind: she tore away at his tunic, which bunched up over his shoulder blades exposing his bruised and wounded muscles.

Regaining his senses, Gwarwyn sought to restrain himself. It was not right to take advantage of their ordeal to abuse this human girl who abhorred him. He flexed his arms and raised his body to walk away. Yet, Anwen pulled him in, and sought to resume their kissing.

The surprising way Anwen was behaving caught Gwarwyn in a surge of desire. They embraced again and then undressed hastily, fingers fumbling over buttons and clasps. When their bodies were freed from all bonds, Gwarwyn seized Anwen's wrists and held her outstretched arms above her head as he entered her.

Joined, they rose and fell in a wild, arrhythmic concert. Their faces pressed against each other, now rubbing tenderly, then bumping at random. At last, they sighed and embraced one last time, eyes closed; they then passed out, dead to the world in their ecstasy. Around them, the rain stopped, the river grew calm, and only the crashing sounds of the falls and the calls of night birds broke the evening silence.

When Gwarwyn rose from her body, it was dawn and the moon was starting to sink below the horizon. He lifted Anwen's head up and brushed her eyelids with the tip of his tongue. Her eyes opened and he kissed her slowly, all urgency gone, savoring the taste of salt, blood and sex in her mouth. As their lips separated, Gwarwyn ran his hands on her wet hair, finally completing the gesture that had initiated their lovemaking.

Gwarwyn reached over his side and groped for his tunic, which he took in both hands and wrung out, releasing as much of the filthy water as he could. He sat on the boulder and found Anwen's own blouse and jerkin, which he wrenched dry and handed over to her, repeating the operation with their trousers. Not a word was exchanged while they were getting dressed.

When he was ready to speak, a multitude of questions assailed him. "What were you doing alone on a raft in the river in the middle of the night?" He asked softly, to avoid sounding reproachful.

She gave a rueful smile. "I was running away from home. I was intending to float only a few hundred yards until I reached the landing at our neighbor's estate, where I meant to steal one of his horses. Once in the raft, I discovered I could not guide it because the current was too strong."

"Why were you running away from home?"

Anwen's reply was full of bitterness. "My father wants me to marry Ormund Rhys, a swine if there ever lived one... I'd rather die than live with him. But, of course, now ..." She broke off.

7

"Now what?" asked Gwarwyn anxiously.

"Now I don't have to worry about marrying him, or anyone else. I hope my father will allow me to hide in a nunnery to wait out the rest of my days. When he dies, I will be free to do as I desire."

"But Anwen," protested Gwarwyn. "I love you and will marry you and will make you forever happy as my mate."

"Me marry YOU?... My family would never consent, and we would face universal rejection. ... And ... me marry an unclean *bwbach*?! How could I live with you, who are not even human? What would happen when we had our first fight and you turned into an evil *boggart* bent on hurting me?" She seemed so vehement in her rejection of the marriage proposal that Gwarwyn did not have time to get offended.

Finally, he shook his head with a grimace. "I would never have hurt you. It's not allowed to those of my kind to commit physical violence upon humans. ..." He tried to say much more, but words stuck in his throat. "But you're right. I am a *bwbach* and can't wed a human. Let's get you back to your family." He helped out of the rock and together they waded towards the bank of the river.

As they got to the shore, their wrenched garments were starting to dry, clinging to their bodies. They halted for a moment to rearrange their clothing.

"Well, we best go on our separate ways," he declared. "I won't tell anyone what happened, but will remember you forever. Please try to be happy."

"I'll have to tell Father that my maidenhood is lost, but won't say it was you who took it. Go in peace." Anwen turned around and started to draw away. Then, suddenly, she came back and kissed his cheek. "I'm sorry. I'll always remember you. You were kinder to me than any man I've known."

She walked away without looking back again.

Gwarwyn sat on the ground, his breast heaving. He had known love and tasted despair. He bent the head on his chest, and uttered a disconsolate moan. The memory of an unrealized dream, of lips that had passionately touched his, would remain with him for a long time.

He glanced around. The morning was advancing and there was not a cloud in the heavens. The Neath ran placidly as it flowed towards the falls.

He gathered his pole and fish basket. His fishing trip had ended leaving him empty-handed and with an ache in his heart. It was time for him to move.

Matias Travieso-Diaz is a retired lawyer, engineer, and failed painter, and a collector of Maria Callas recordings. He believes the best things in life are opera, jazz, Italian food and vino. Matias lives in Alexandria, Virginia, with his daughter, two dogs and a world class inventory of weeds.

The Inspector and The Lady

by David Dixon

A t his desk beside the fireplace in the back room of the customs house, Reid yawned. *Laws Concerning the Import of Magical Items, As Amended by the Seventh Council* was hardly enchanting reading, and he hadn't slept well the night before. He rarely did these days. Dreams had plagued him over the past month, as if the battle had been yesterday instead of fifteen years ago.

The bell above the door in the front room clanged. Reid glanced over his shoulder at the small window set into the stone, closed tight against the cold. With any luck, whatever his visitor needed would take the rest of the daylight, and he had a strict prohibition against reading by candlelight. He smiled, glad for the interruption—until he heard the all-too-familiar high, clear voice from the front.

"Chief Inspector!" the voice called. "Chief inspector!"

Great Lord of Fire and Smoke, it's her again.

He stood from his desk reluctantly, smoothing his shirt, retying his purple cravat to close its high collar, and draping the sash of his office from his right shoulder to his left hip with deliberate slowness.

He looked about the room for any further reason to delay going up front. His eyes settled on his ceremonial saber in its ornate sheath and belt, rarely worn, but still technically a badge of his office. He cinched it around his waist, then reflexively smoothed his shirt yet again, a nervous tic in the face of unpleasant business he'd developed over the years.

He opened the heavy wooden door and stepped into the anteroom. The young woman standing at the counter was a familiar sight even though he'd only known her for a few unfortunate months. She was short and lithe with dark, piercing eyes framed by even darker eyebrows which stood out against her pale skin and matched the shock of raven-black hair peeking out from under her cowl. Her cloak was rich burgundy velvet trimmed in ermine, and she wore it over a deep blue dress in the imperial style favored by the city's wealthy. Reid thought of her as a creeping rosebush—brightly colored, impossible to get rid of, and full of thorns.

He silently cursed himself for letting his assistant Artis have the day off. He preferred it when he had a buffer between himself and the citizens' complaints—especially this citizen.

"Lady Maya, how might I be of service?" Reid forced out as politely as he could.

"I warned you last week the *Woken Furies* was captained by a brigand, and I told you when it docked here, there would be nothing but trouble."

He sighed. "Yes, my lady, you did. And I believe I informed *you* last week that His Majesty has given me writ to enforce the law, not the whims of individual merchants, and that, further, having no writ against the captain of the *Woken Furies*, I would not prevent him from making a port call here."

Her eyes narrowed. "Mock me all you like, Chief Inspector. But inspect *this*, and tell me I was wrong."

She produced a vial of crimson liquid from her left pocket. He held out his palm, and she extended a manicured hand to drop the vial in it. He pinched the glass between his thumb and forefinger, lifting it toward the wan light streaming through the customs house windows. The color shifted subtly as he rotated it, and on a hunch he turned it on its side in his hand. The crimson disappeared into pitch black. When he straightened it up again, the red color returned. Stamped in the cork was a trapper's seal marked *Gryphon blood, grade 1*. He pulled off the stopper and sniffed.

The wet odor of rotting wood filled his nostrils at first, followed by an acrid tang that almost brought tears to his eyes. Gryphon blood. He restoppered it, looked across the counter at her, and shrugged.

Lady Maya crossed her arms across her chest and gave Reid a glare that struck him with the fury of a winter's gale bearing down on a lonely lighthouse.

He wondered what he'd done to deserve this, this persistent little thorn in his side, with her seemingly inexhaustible supply of complaints and equally inexhaustible energy to pursue them. Maybe it was just the impudence of youth. Had he been this demanding in his early twenties? Perhaps. He gave her a perfect smile of bureaucratic indifference, just so she wouldn't think she was getting to him.

"Well?" he asked. "The ship has been docked for four days and if her captain was selling his wares without paying his duties, I'd have heard about it by now. After all, you are hardly the only purveyor of—"

"You think I'm just some rich girl with too much time on her hands who doesn't want competition for her business, don't you?" she asked.

"Nothing could be further from the truth," Reid lied.

"Liar," she interrupted. "Give me that back and I'll show you what I mean."

Reid forced himself not to scowl as he handed the vial to her. She placed it on the counter and withdrew another vial from pocket, this one full of a shiny liquid.

"Quicksilver," she explained. "Now, what happens when gryphon's blood and quicksilver are mixed?"

"I am a customs inspector, my lady, not an alchemist."

"Nothing happens," she said. "Quicksilver and gryphon blood are nonreactive. Surely you know that."

"Why, exactly, would I know that?"

"No wonder you're such a terrible inspector," she muttered as she dropped a spot of the blood onto the counter. Next she opened her vial of quicksilver, but before she poured it, she nodded at his saber. "You might want to be ready."

Reid blinked. Was she seriously suggesting he would need his sword when she—

A single drop of shimmering quicksilver hit the gryphon blood, and a coil of thick black smoke rose towards the ceiling, materializing into a snakelike head and scaled neck. Its mouth opened, a maw of serrated fangs. Heart in his throat, Reid drew his saber, but the creature struck at him first.

He lost his footing and tumbled backwards into the wall of register books with a shout.

The massive snake loomed over him, preparing a blow it couldn't miss. He winced but there was the flash of a blade and the top half of the creature vanished into smoke, even as another pair of long necks began reforming out of the original spot on the desk. Next to the desk, Lady Maya held a thin knife in one hand—produced from where, he had no idea—and a large vial of a wicked-looking green liquid in the other.

"I *told* you to be ready!" she shouted.

She doused the smoke with green liquid from her vial and suddenly the office was quiet again.

Reid's heart hammered against his ribs as he stared at Lady Maya.

Her eyes narrowed in satisfaction. "Now do you believe me? *Now?*"

He managed a nod and got to his feet. "What was that thing?"

"It's good you're a customs inspector and not a soldier. I told you to be ready, didn't I? That *thing* was a Torinthian hydra," Lady Maya said. "That vial I gave you is hydra's blood, not gryphon's blood, which is an entirely predictable turn of events that could have been avoided if you'd listened to my warnings about the *Woken Furies* and her captain." She stared daggers at him. "But you didn't."

Reid took a deep breath to calm himself and resheathed his saber before he spoke. "First off, I *was* a soldier once upon a time and a damned good one, thank you, but that was over a decade ago, and I wasn't expecting to have to fight a hydra in my office. A bit more warning besides 'be ready' would have been useful. Secondly, your complaint about *Woken Furies* was hardly better—you made it seem like he had some underworld contacts somewhere else and might be able to undercut your prices because of it, which is hardly my purview. Not that he was bringing in…" Reid fumbled for the right words as the magnitude of the situation slowly dawned on him. "Bringing in… enough hydra blood to… to…"

"Destroy the whole city?" Lady Maya finished, arching an eyebrow at him. "I'm glad you've grasped the situation. Since you do, perhaps you should impound his cargo before any more of it gets into circulation?"

His blood ran cold. "How much of it is already sold? How much—"

"Fortunately, I have the only sample," Lady Maya said, her eyebrows knitting together as she glowered at him. "And it's a good thing I got it, apparently, since if it were up to the king's officers, the city would shortly be in ruins."

Her words stung, but Reid had more important things to deal with than insults. "Come with me," he told her as he slipped past her towards the door. "Let's visit your *Woken Furies*."

He pushed the door open, and she followed him into the chilly street. The wind blew, carrying with it snowflakes and a biting cold that seemed to seep right into his bones. He shuddered, but there was no time to grab his cloak. The terrifying thought of a crop of hydras teeming from alchemical shops citywide and wreaking havoc on every other corner was more than enough to make him forget the weather. He took off at a rapid clip towards the docks. Lady Maya stayed close behind him, letting him clear a path through the cobblestoned streets as merchants, nobles, tradesmen, and the city's riffraff alike scattered out of his way. After all, no one wanted to deal with a customs official unless it was absolutely necessary, especially not an unusually perturbed and hurried one.

When they emerged from the rows of narrow buildings lining the waterfront and onto the wharfs, Reid paused, casting a glance over his shoulder. Lady Maya was right on his heels, her cheeks rosy as she huffed breaths of condensation into the frigid air. Her dark eyes glittered with something close to respect, for once.

"It's that one with the red trim and the black mainsail." She pointed to a ship up the wharf. "The vials of hydra blood are in a pair of chests in the hold."

"Pray it's still there," Reid muttered, striding towards the ship.

"It's good to be taken seriously. And to see you move so quickly on my behalf, for once," she said, matching his stride.

I assure you, me moving this fast has everything to do with hydras and nothing to do with you. "Well, my lady, it is my policy to take all credible complaints seriously. Yours or anyone else's."

"Ha! You dragged your feet last week when I told you Shimone had missed his deadline to register that monstrosity of an—"

"He was one day late, and he'd already discussed it with me," Reid interrupted. "Besides, it was hardly any concern of yours, save that he was a competitor."

"That has nothing to do with it," she sniffed. "I just care about the law. Seems like you should too, given that's your royal charter." She finished with a charming smile that in different circumstances Reid would have found positively intriguing, but now found maddening instead.

"Oh, is that the case?" he asked. "Well then you should know that displaying alchemical goods outside before sunrise is a violation of the Royal Ordinance Concerning Magical Sales. Section thirty-two, second paragraph, if you're looking for the citation." It was his turn to smile. "If I recall correctly, you've had three Wigun pelts on display outside before sunup twice this week."

She reddened. "Wigun pelts aren't alchemical, and—"

"The Royal Alchemical Registry says differently, my lady," Reid said. "You are no doubt familiar with—"

She grabbed his arm and twisted him to face her, a surprising amount of strength in her grip. Her dark eyes blazed. "Don't mock me. I'm familiar with it. My brother helped write it. I won't display them before sunrise again, but don't—"

"You said you wish to be taken seriously and not ignored. So I won't. If you'd like my attention, I'll be glad to give it to you," Reid snapped.

They walked in silence until they reached *Woken Furies*. Five crewmembers stared sullenly down at them from the top of the gangplank.

"Sir Reid of Falstrop, His Majesty's Chief Customs Inspector, coming aboard," Reid announced.

"*Reid*," Lady Maya murmured. "Be careful."

A tall, thin young man in a stylish blue topcoat appeared at the top of the gangplank before she could finish. With his rakish good looks and blonde hair, Reid thought he looked more like a minor lord at court than a ship captain.

"Chief Inspector, welcome aboard! I am Captain Harker, master of this fair vessel, and—" Harker's eyes widened and a grin lit his face. "Why, Lady Maya, what a *surprise*." He paused, as if savoring his words. After our last parting, I was unaware that you wished to speak to me further, but I am glad to see you've changed your mind."

"I haven't, not one whit," Lady Maya snapped. "In fact, I do not wish to speak to you even now. I am here only out of necessity."

Reid couldn't say for sure what their issue was, but given the similarity in their ages as well as the vehemence in Lady Maya's voice, he could guess. But that wasn't his concern. He strode up the gangplank, Lady Maya close on his heels.

"What seems to be the trouble?" Harker asked.

"I have reason to believe that you have counterfeit cargo aboard, which you intend to sell in contrivance of the law."

"Illegal cargo?" Harker sputtered. "Why, I never... I've nothing illegal at all aboard, good sir, and—"

"I said nothing of illegality, Captain Harker," Reid said, stifling a smile. "I said 'counterfeit.' 'Counterfeit' only becomes 'illegal' if you sell it, which I hope for your sake hasn't happened. I'm sure you'd never do such a thing intentionally. In fact, I'm looking out for you, because I fear you have been duped by your supplier into selling hydra's blood as counterfeit gryphon's blood. That would highly illegal. The punishment would be..." Reid shrugged. "Who knows, exactly? But I imagine the best you could hope for would be the loss your

18

berthing privileges, and at worst—if there were deaths or damage?—you'd probably hang. So I'm sure you won't mind me examining your cargo. Agreed?"

Harker frowned. "Chief Inspector, you are correct. I would never, of course, knowingly violate His Majesty's laws, and I will rectify this posthaste if it is as you say. Perhaps we could discuss this further in my quarters?"

Don't want your men to know how much trouble they might be in, do you? Smart boy.

"Of course, Captain Harker," Reid said graciously. "Lady Maya here will accompany me. She has an alchemical aptitude I lack and can help test the reliability of the claims made against your cargo by an anonymous informant."

Captain Harker's mouth twitched, and his eyes flicked to Lady Maya. "Of course. Lady Maya is a woman of much aptitude, in a variety of areas." The look of hatred on her face could have laid waste to half the city, but she didn't answer. Reid glared at Harker, but the captain had already turned on his heel to lead them aft.

They followed him below decks through a dim, narrow passage, pausing only long enough for Harker to exchange a word with one of his men, who nodded and disappeared down a ladder to the ship's hold. The captain's quarters turned out to be spacious, drafty, and well-lit by large windows set into the ship's rear bulkhead.

"Please, make yourselves comfortable," Harker said as he gestured towards chairs arranged around a small felt-covered table bolted to the deck. "I shall speak with my quartermaster, and we'll fetch the gryphon's blood. I apologize for the chill, but perhaps a glass of port would warm you up?" He turned to Lady Maya and gave her an exaggerated nod. "Do you still prefer tawny ports, my lady?"

She didn't answer, and instead sat in one of the chairs with a huff.

"I'll take that as a yes," Harker said. He fetched a bottle from a wine rack mounted against the wall pulled out the cork with a deep *thunk*. He set it on the table alongside three glasses, bowed, and left Reid and Lady Maya alone.

Reid settled into a chair and poured two glasses.

"I told you he was a scoundrel and a brigand," she seethed. "And now he's got you in here while he no doubt filches some samples of real gryphon's blood so that—"

"No doubt he is a scoundrel," Reid said with a droll smile. "Although I suspect you know more about that side of him than I do. As to whether he is a brigand? Perhaps. I'll know soon enough."

"Why?"

"When he comes back and sees me drinking, he'll I'm ready to buy whatever lie he's selling. By the time he discovers I haven't, it will be too late, but until then we may as well enjoy his port."

She sighed but picked up the glass he'd poured her and drank it without looking at him.

"I suppose you've dined at this table before?" Reid asked.

"I don't want to talk about it." Any trace of her earlier cheer vanished.

How did a lady like you wind up involved with a shining example of villainy like Captain Harker here? Reid thought as he sipped his port and looked across the table at Lady Maya's sharp, frowning features.

He knew better than to ask.

The stateroom door opened and Captain Harker arrived with three crewmen in tow. The first thing Reid noticed were the cutlasses on their belts. Despite the cold, a bead of sweat formed on his forehead.

Surely, they wouldn't attempt violence against one of the king's officers—not when a hundred passersby had seen him board the ship, and not when they that violence against an officer of the crown was punished by drawing and quartering. And Captain Harker was Lady Maya's former lover. He wouldn't hurt *her* would he?

"Thank you for the port, Captain Harker," Reid said coolly as he stood. "I hope there won't be any trouble." He laid a hand as casually as he dared on the pommel of his sword. Lady Maya hadn't moved from her spot at the table, but her eyes flicked between Reid's sword and the crew's cutlasses.

"No trouble at all, Chief Inspector," Harker said. "Now, please, sit back down and keep your hand off your blade." Reid did neither. "There's no need for it. I promise. You see, I had my quartermaster test the gryphon's blood. And it's hydra blood, just like you said." He turned to Lady Maya. "I'm not sure how you obtained a sample so quickly yourself, but bravo." He bowed theatrically. "I really was unaware, and I assure you, I *will* have words—more than words—with my supplier."

Hakwer's honesty stunned Reid, and he almost relaxed. Captains, even the honest ones, were rarely so forthcoming with customs agents.

"*But...*" Captain Harker added with a grimace, the word hanging in the air like a match about to light a cannon.

Reid gripped his saber.

"No, no, no, Chief Inspector, *please*," Harker pleaded. "This is a problem swordplay won't solve: the ship's owner wants a return on his investment, and that gryphon's blood is a substantial portion of that investment. I can't let you take it from me. I have to sell it."

"I can't let you—" Reid began.

"I know, and that's the problem," Harker said. "But fortunately, I foresaw this difficulty, and I served you both a... special variety of port. Laced with an interesting compound of lotus extract, ginseng, and a few other ingredients."

Reid could hear his heartbeat in his ears. "You *poisoned* us? You bastard," he sputtered. "You're going to hang from the highest—"

"No," Lady Maya whispered from the table. "Not poison. An anti-mnemonic—a forgetfulness potion."

Harker smiled. "Precisely. Just a little nightcap for the mind. So, if you two don't mind, you can stay right here in my quarters for another quarter hour or so until it takes effect, then I'll be glad to let the both of you off unharmed—if a bit confused—with no harm done. For the time being, anyway."

"And if not?" Reid growled.

Harker's face fell. "I would hate for you to choose that route, Chief Inspector. You I'm ambivalent about, but I would truly regret hurting Lady Maya here." He nodded toward his men and their cutlasses. "Your choice."

Reid collapsed into his chair. He couldn't fight his way out, and he wouldn't consign both himself and Lady Maya to death. "We'll wait."

"I thought as much," Harker said. He flipped a small hourglass over and pointed to the blue sand that trickled to the bottom globe. "When it's done, I'll let you leave, although you won't remember me telling you that. Don't frown so! It's better than the alternative."

With that, he followed his men out of the room and slammed the door closed behind him. A key turned in the lock, and Reid and Lady Maya were alone again.

"Damn him," Reid muttered as he leapt from his seat.

"I *told* you he was a brigand."

"Again, you crowing about being right both after the fact and after you failed to fully convey the true magnitude of the situation is most unhelpful," he snapped.

"You're the one that keeps not listening," she snapped back. "You're the one who always thinks you know best and won't pay attention when I warn you. You think I'm just some pretty little thing who doesn't know what she's talking about, and so you humor me instead of actually listening. This is *your* fault."

"Oh really?" Reid asked, searching the room for something to write on before the potion took hold. "This is my fault? What would your plan have been?"

"I don't know," she answered. "That's not my job. *You're* the king's officer."

Reid ignored her jibe and attempted to pull open the drawers in Harker's desk, but they were locked. He drew his saber and slipped the blade between the desk and the drawer, planning to pry it open. There had to be a quill and ink inside.

"It won't work," Lady Maya said. "They're enchanted."

"We'll see about that." Reid grunted as he pressed his weight against the saber. The desk drawer didn't budge.

"I *said* it won't work," Lady Maya said. "But don't listen to me if you don't want to. I've only been right every time so far."

"There's more than one way into a drawer." Reid brought the blade high above the desk and aimed a massive stroke at one of the desk edges, intending to split the wood, allowing him access to the drawer beneath. The blow glanced off without leaving so much as a scratch.

Her lips curved up in the faintest hint of a smile. "Are you finished? Because I have something that might actually work."

"I could scratch something into the table and—"

"Not unless you carry the table out with you," she interrupted. "Our memories will be so befuddled when the potion takes hold we won't remember much beyond our names and what we ate for breakfast."

Reid sighed. "Fine. What's *your* plan then?"

"I thought you'd never ask," she muttered as she unbuttoned her heavy, fur-trimmed cloak and shrugged it off to reveal the form-fitting bodice of her dress. Reid noticed her figure and couldn't help but think that had it belonged to anybody else besides the condescending, bothersome Lady Maya, he'd have been interested in seeing more of it. But what truly captured his attention were the dozens of tiny vials in the equally tiny pockets sewn into her cloak.

She withdrew a few vials and placed them in a row on the table, then studied them for a moment before her lips drew into a frown. "I try to be prepared. But my preparations are usually aimed at encouraging sales, not counteracting criminal plots."

He didn't like the sound of that. "What exactly does that mean?"

"That means," she began as she plucked four vials off the table one by one, "that I don't have what I need to counteract his potion. And unfortunately, we're running out of time before we start forgetting." She pointed to the glass, its sand continuing to mound in the bottom globe.

"Are you *sure* you don't have what you need?"

She glared at him. "Of course. I'm the best alchemist in the city—if I say I don't have it, I don't."

"Gods damn him," Reid muttered. "If Harker gets away with this I'll never forgive myself. That is, if I could remember he'd done it." His mood grew fouler at the thought.

She studied her ingredients. "Foxglove as a concentrator, good… Now, if I just had a tincture of juniper," she murmured. "But without it? Hmmm… I wonder… No, that won't do…"

Reid scanned the room again, looking for some way out. His eye settled on the wine rack.

A tincture of juniper.

Juniper.

He scrambled across the stateroom and pulled one bottle after another out of the wine rack, checking the labels.

"What are you doing?" she asked. "What could you—" Her eyes widened.

"That's right. *Gin.*" Reid grinned. He held out a dark bottle with an ornate label reading *Alscott's Gin, distilled of grain and*

*infused with juniper, coriander, rose, myrtle, and sundry spices according to
Lord Alscott's famous recipe.*

"Perfect!" Lady Maya enthused, a wide smile lighting up
her face.

"And it's not just any gin, it's Alscott's," he said. "This
bottle would cost you half my salary for a month."

"All the better it's expensive," Lady Maya said. "Serves the
bastard right."

Reid sat the bottle on the table next to her vials. "Now,
answer me this: what made you suspect he brought in hydra's
blood masquerading as griffin's blood?"

She didn't take her eyes off the potion she was mixing as
she answered, her voice quiet and embarrassed. "He's a crook
and a rogue, and he always has been. I found him charming,
once, in a flight of foolish fancy. But he proved more of a
scoundrel than I knew, and I was serious when I said I never
wanted to see him again. But before that, when we were
more… friendly, I suppose, he told me had a plan to make a
fortune of gryphon's blood because he'd found a new supplier,
but none of what he told me made sense. I suspected fraud, but
I figured he was in on the scheme. I certainly didn't know it was
hydra blood, and I believe him when he says he didn't either.
Anyway, the day he docked, I paid a crewmember to filch me a
sample. I couldn't believe what happened when I tested it, so I
went straight to you—straight to the authorities, I mean."

"And here we are," Reid mused, frowning at the mixture
she'd poured into one of the unused wine glasses.

Lady Maya unstoppered the bottle of gin and took a glance
at the label and her face paled. "Oh no. Oh no. Oh *no*," she
murmured.

Reid's heart sank. "What now?"

She pressed her lips together and before she answered.
"There will be some unfortunate… side effects. Because this
isn't just a tincture of juniper. It's got coriander as well and I

have no idea how much, but if it's as much as I suspect it's going to make us very drowsy. If we don't keep talking, we'll likely pass out on the—"

"If Harker comes back and finds us passed out, he'll know we've done something to ourselves and probably pitch us asleep into the harbor. We'll be sleeping in the Halls of the Shadow King for all eternity." Reid's face darkened.

"Yes," she said, fidgeting with a potion vial in each hand. "But that's not all."

He groaned. "What else?"

"Rose. And myrtle," she prompted.

"I'm a customs inspector. Not an alchemist, as you take great pains to point out."

"Rose petal is an aphrodisiac."

He felt his ears turning red. "And myrtle?"

Lady Maya looked away. "Myrtle is an incredibly *powerful* aphrodisiac."

For a moment, the room was as silent as a crypt.

"Ah."

"Yes."

Reid coughed, doing his best to ignore the thousand questions swirling in his brain. "And there's no other way to…"

She shook her head.

"So. Which one of us drinks?"

"We both do," she said. "We can't trust Captain Harker will let us both go unharmed. Both of us drinking doubles the chances that one of us can go get help."

"You're *sure* there's nothing else we can…" He trailed off as she splashed the gin into the wine glass. The previously clear mixture turned a deep shade of violet.

"It's either drink or lose your memory and Harker gets away," Lady Maya said, voice trembling as she put the glass to her lips. She swallowed half the potion with a grimace and passed it to Reid. He sighed and drank the remainder down. It tasted of rotting pine needles and blood.

"I would've thought Alscott's, would taste better," he rasped. He waited a moment for some magical feeling, but nothing happened. "I don't feel anything. Are you sure it worked?"

"Just wait for it," she said as she put her vials of ingredients back into her hidden pockets.

"And you're sure it will take effect before we lose our memory of—" It hit him like a blow to the back of the head.

His body begged for sleep as if he'd not slept in days. The world fuzzed and slipped out of focus. It took all the strength he had to keep his eyes open, and he feared if he blinked he'd never open them.

"It… it hit me," he announced.

"Y-y-yes," she stammered. "There must've been more… coriander than… I expected. But we cannot fall asleep. We… can't."

He knew what she meant, but in his mind, Reid found the idea of curling up with her and falling asleep the most desirable thing in the world.

"Don't look at me… like… that," she warned.

"Like what?" he asked, admiring the way her dark hair framed her face and noticing the slim lines of her lithe frame just before she wrapped back up in her cloak and.

"Like you are right now," she answered. "Like… like you want me to put my head on your chest and lean against you and go to… sleep. I know what you're thinking."

Even through his magical exhaustion, he couldn't help but smile.

"That's not what I was thinking. I think that's what *you* were thinking. But now that you mention it, it doesn't sound so bad, does it?"

She looked away. "Don't let the aphrodisiac fool you. You don't really like me. Like I said before, you think I'm just a young, pretty face you don't have to take seriously."

"That's not true. I mean, you *are* very pretty," Reid admitted before he could stop himself. "And I do take you seriously. I'd be fool not to. You're quite sharp. This potion is proof. And I swear, sometimes I think you know the city's codes better than I do."

"Thank you. For what it's worth, I appreciate that you actually have taken action on my complaints. Especially considering how many I've lodged."

"There have been a lot. Almost as if complaints about minor infractions aren't the real purpose of your visits." Reid's felt a blissful smile cross face in a detached sort of way, as if it weren't really him in his own body.

This stuff is strong. Don't be a fool, old boy.

"You presume much, Chief Inspector," she said. "What other purpose could I have? Do you think I would bother an officer of the king with petty things just to get his attention?"

Something in her tone—as if she were less refuting his charge than reveling in it—made Reid pause. He studied her with renewed interest before he answered with a smile. "I would never presume to understand why you might do something like that. Although, perhaps, having been disappointed by Captain Harker, so close to your own age, you decided to pursue someone older. Perhaps your visits were just an excuse."

"An excuse for what?" her dark eyes had a curious, almost guilty, gleam in them. Reid wondered why he'd never noticed how deep and inviting those eyes were until now.

"Perhaps you wanted an excuse to talk to the Chief Inspector."

As soon as the words left his mouth, he felt himself go red. *Damn this potion. Damn it, damn it.*

Lady Maya swallowed whatever she was going to say. She stood and looked away from him a moment, then turned back to him. "Given the nature of the potion and this... conversation, perhaps we would be better off not talking."

"I agree, my lady," Reid answered, glad she'd let him off so easily.

Although he still wondered if perhaps there wasn't something to his idea. And if there *were* something to it, wouldn't that mean that... She'd pestered him long before there was any sort of aphrodisiac potion involved, after all. It wasn't like he'd dreamt up all the other minor issues she'd come to his office about before this one.

He realized with a pang of embarrassment that he'd been staring at her the entire time. He looked away.

She *was* quite smart. Her understanding of some of the Eighth Council's decisions on trade law would have shamed many a court solicitor, and he'd heard nothing but praises for her alchemical skill and business acumen.

And she was beautiful, he could finally allow himself to admit.

So *of course* he'd feel this way about her, under the influence of an aphrodisiac. He needed to think of something else—anything. He closed his eyes to think of...

He felt himself falling and woke with a start, head almost hitting the table. He pushed himself back from the table and stood unsteadily. Across from him, Lady Maya's eyes drooped and she swayed on her feet.

"Lady Maya!" he barked, and her eyes snapped open.

"Maybe we *should* talk," she said, rubbing her face. "Just not about... anything that might relate to... well... us."

Her phrasing made him blink. "Is there an *us* to talk about?" *Pull yourself together, damn it.* "My apologies. I... this... well, you understand," he said, struggling to keep from wondering what it would be like to have her on his arm at one of the many court functions he was invited to and never attended. He imagined her in popular court fashion, the line of her neck as it met her shoulders, her delicate collarbones revealed in a dress with a scooping neckline.

She gave him an odd sort of look—half a frown as if she could tell what he was thinking about, but at the same time, half a smile as if she wanted to be upset with him but couldn't. He did his best to keep an even expression.

"I do understand, but we've got to talk, else we'll pass out for sure," she warned, her hand covering her mouth as she yawned. "So think of something interesting."

"My lady, I am a customs inspector," Reid said. "I'm afraid interesting is not my line of work."

Her mouth twitched into a tiny smile. "Fine, Chief Inspector. I'll ask you questions until I find something interesting. After all, there has to be *something* interesting under there, right?" She nodded at the sash that marked him as the king's officer.

The words seemed to slip out before he could stop them. "All kinds of interesting things, my lady."

She swallowed before she spoke, and he couldn't keep his eyes off her delicate neck. "You said when we came aboard that you were *Sir* Reid. I didn't know that. I never knew you to be a knight," she said, and he breathed a little easier. He didn't like talking about his title, but at least the topic wouldn't get him in trouble.

I'm never touching rose petals again if I live through this.

"I only use my title when I need to," he said. "Sometimes it helps encourage compliance. It's nothing really."

Her eyebrows rose. "Most men I know wouldn't hesitate to refer to themselves as *Sir* every chance they got."

"Most men have probably done more to earn theirs than I did. Like I said, it's nothing."

"I have known plenty of vain men knighted for very little," Lady Maya said. "What were you knighted for? Stopping some lucrative scheme to get around the King's tariffs? Enforcing a record number of tax duties?"

"No. It was years before I became an inspector, much less the chief inspector." Reid sighed. "For action at Stonyford Bridge. It's not much of a story, really. I was very young, and—"

"My father rode to the relief of Stonyford Bridge!" Lady Maya interrupted, her eyes wide. "He told me later he'd never seen such bravery as he saw among its defenders. Sir Garwin and Lord LeMont made their entire careers at court off their exploits at Stonyford."

Reid shrugged. "They can glory in it all they want. For my part, I never want to see such slaughter again, and I certainly have no intention of making a career out of it. When he knighted me, His Majesty gave me the opportunity to continue to serve the crown, but I had no intention of it being under arms. Never again." He patted the saber by his side. "And this hardly counts."

He looked across the table at her and waited for the next inevitable, disappointing, infuriating question, the one he hated hearing—the one that always came.

She tilted her head at him, eyes penetrating but with an understanding in them that he hadn't expected. "My father said the fighting at Stonyford Bridge was the worst carnage he'd ever seen. Is it difficult? I mean, living with all that?" she asked softly.

He blinked in surprise. The question she gave him was *not* the one he expected, but something altogether different, a question that treated him like a *man* and not like a knight or a hero. He almost didn't know what to say, but he stammered out an answer anyway. "Not most days. But some." He nodded, more to himself than to her. "Some days certainly are."

She didn't say anything for a moment, but then they spoke simultaneously.

"I—"

"No—"

They stared at one another for a moment, and there was such an understanding and compassion in her eyes that Reid felt he could have kissed her. He rubbed his face to try to wipe away the thoughts. "Go on, my lady. What were you going to say?"

"I was going to apologize for bringing it up. Had I known, I wouldn't have. I'm sorry."

"It's all right," Reid said. "You're the first person to ever ask me how I felt about that day, believe it or not. Most want to know what exactly I did on that blood-slicked bridge, what terrible role I had in that godsforsaken battle. As if I'd want to relive it, to tell them of the joy and laughter and youth we stole from each other over that cursed river—when both sides were just boys exactly the same except we'd been born on opposite banks." He finished more fiercely than he'd intended, and he nursed the sudden pang of concern that he'd upset her, but when his eyes met hers, he found sadness, not distaste.

"I think that's a ghastly question for anyone ask, and I think it's noble of you to not make a career out of that day," Lady Maya whispered. "I've known many a prouder man to boast of far less. But pride doesn't make them better men." She paused, and Reid opened his mouth to reply, but she kept talking. "I think I… I'm growing fond of you, Chief Inspector."

"I'm fond of you too, Lady Maya," he said before he could stop himself. He tried not to look at her, but there was no way to avoid it. Their gazes met. Her eyes looked like deep caves he couldn't live without exploring, and her rosy cheeks and pink lips called to him in a language he couldn't ignore. Her eyes flicked to the floor for a second, but then returned to his, a desperate pleading in them as plain as the sun in the sky—but she wasn't pleading him to stay away. It was quite the opposite.

He took a step around the table closer to her, drawn by some magnetism he was powerless to resist. He closed the distance to her in an eyeblink and took her hands into his, which he clasped to his chest, rubbing her fingers to keep them warm. He brought her hands to his lips and kissed them softly. He'd never felt anything as wonderful as her skin on his lips. She sighed, and he let them go so he could cradle her head in his hands. She put her arms around him and looked up at him with such a yearning that he couldn't stop himself. He pulled her tightly to him and leaned down.

The tromp of heavy boots outside the doorway startled them both, and they parted, her fingers trailing across his chest as they returned to opposite sides of the table. Reid shook his head to try to push out all the thoughts of how wonderful their kiss would have been. The key turned in the lock.

He glanced at the hourglass and watched the final grains of blue sand trickle from the top globe. Harker stepped inside, his grin wide and jovial.

"Still doing all right, my friends?"

"I—I think so," Lady Maya answered, brow furrowed like she was desperately trying to capture some fleeting thought. "Although I feel a bit... odd. I can't seem to remember anything we discussed. I think I'd rather like to sit down." She sat unsteadily, taking Harker's offered hand as he helped her into her chair.

Harker's smile grew wider. "Bah. It was nothing really. I apologize. You must've drunk a little too much port. But I'm sure the Chief Inspector here has a stronger constitution. You no doubt remember our agreement?"

Reid blinked, feigning confusion. "Our... agreement? I can't say as I do. My apologies. This is most unusual, Captain

Harker. To tell you the truth, I don't know if I'd have remembered your name had Lady Maya here not said it."

"Oh my, Chief Inspector." Had Reid not known better he would have thought concern on the Captain's face was genuine. I'll have to drink some of that port myself, it seems! Must be quite the good stuff. You and I discussed berthing costs for next year, remember? You promised to send a letter the moment the Ministry published the rates."

Reid frowned, then pretended to pretend to remember, knowing Harker would expect him to agree if only to avoid embarrassment. "Oh, yes, of course, berthing rates. I'll certainly send you that letter as soon as I hear."

"Excellent, Chief Inspector." Harker clapped him on the back. "And if there's anything you ever need from me, don't hesitate to trot back down here." The captain's eyes strayed to the bottle of gin on the table, and Reid's heart skipped a beat.

Gods damn it, why didn't I put it back? If he figures out she's crafted a potion, he'll slit our throats for sure. Gods damn it.

Harker picked up the bottle with an amused smile on his face. "Ha! Perhaps *this* is why you two are feeling the effects so much. Not the port but the *gin*. You two sure do like your spirits, don't you?" He snorted. "I do have a confession, though: though, this isn't really Alscott's. It's some rotgut gin I picked up by the barrel in Cottesdan and had relabeled. Quite a profit."

Reid did his best to seem confused, and Lady Maya cocked her head.

Harker chuckled as he read the label. "Let's see... *infused with juniper, coriander, rose, myrtle, and sundry spices according to Lord Alscott's famous recipe.* Ha! Lord Alscott would roll over in his grave if he knew this swill had his name on it. I'm sure there's some juniper in here, because it's gin, after all, and I know the schemers that made this stuff bought some coriander off of me, so there's probably some of that as well, but rose petals?

Myrtle? 'Sundry spices?'" Harker snorted. "If there's any of that in there, I'm a monk."

Reid's eyes widened and he looked across the table at Lady Maya, who'd turned almost beet red.

"Now, now, Chief Inspector, don't get upset." Harker tutted. "You won't remember anyway. In fact, I'm afraid you'll find this whole day rather cloudy, when you look back on it."

Reid felt he should at least pretend he was trying to remember. "You're wrong. I'll remember, Captain... Captain, uh..."

"Don't worry, Chief Inspector, I won't hold it against you," Harker said with a comforting hand on his shoulder. "Now, off with the both of you. Lots to do, I'm sure."

Harker hustled Reid and Lady Maya—who still hadn't looked at him—out of his stateroom and back above decks, then to the bottom of the gangplank.

"Farewell," Harker said with a bow. "Don't be strangers!"

He strode back up the gangplank. Reid turned to look at Lady Maya, but she gave a nearly imperceptible shake of her head.

"Don't say anything," he hissed. "Just follow my lead."

She lurched towards the row of shops in front of them—Reid noticed she never reached out for his steadying hand—and he followed. She meandered as if she didn't know where she was going, and he did the same, although he gathered she was making for the alley toward the nearest Royal Guard barracks.

He knew he needed to clear his head, knew he needed to be ready to explain to the Captain of the Guard that Captain Harker had to be arrested, and be ready to lead the Guard back to *Woken Furies* to storm their way aboard if necessary. He knew there was the potential for a battle on the docks if Harker chose to defend his ship. He knew all that, but instead, all he could think about was Harker's revelation about the gin.

If there was no rose or myrtle in the gin, then there was no aphrodisiac. And if there was no aphrodisiac… Did she really feel that way?

He didn't really have to ask.

He knew the answer, as sure as he knew anything.

Yes.

But only once they were out of eyesight from the *Woken Furies* and stopped in front of the Guard barracks did he touch her elbow. She spun to face him. They stared into each other's eyes for a moment before she whispered to him.

"You don't have to—"

His arms wrapped around her and hers around him in the sweetest embrace he'd ever felt. He kissed her desperately.

She kissed back.

David Dixon lives in Springfield, Virginia. His previous publishing credits include three science fiction novellas published by Dark Brew Press and short stories published in *Common Tongue Magazine* and *Wyldblood* (UK).

Periphery

by Laura J. Campbell

"Ichabod," Dr. Hester Percival greeted Ichabod Pob, assuming she was establishing rapport with her patient.

Dr. Percival was making a mistake.

"Don't ever call me that!" Ichabod exploded. "I don't care that you work for my defense attorney; I can't stand attorneys or psychiatrists. Stupid b…" He stopped, mid-misogyny, as he saw a little shadow scamper across the floor, taunting him as it disappeared. "You call me 'Mr. Pob.' I'm old enough to be your grandfather. Although I bet that I'm a lot better looking than your grandfather."

"I am sensing some hostility."

"No shit. Three degrees and that's all you got? I always knew I was better off without one of those."

"You want respect, you show me respect," she demanded. "After all, I am here to help *you* with your defense."

"I don't need you for anything; I don't need *any* woman for anything. In fact, I want my rib back," Ichabod patted his lower left rib-cage, "A little touch-up under the external oblique would be nice."

Hester stopped talking. Without any further hesitation, she picked up her notebooks and pens, gathered up her laptop computer, and left the room.

A guard entered, to take Mr. Pob back to his cell.

"That's how you show you're the boss," he told the guard triumphantly.

***

"You have a visitor" were not the words Ichabod expected to hear.

Everybody had abandoned Ichabod. They couldn't handle him. They were all too weak. That was the problem with the world: there weren't many real men like him left.

That made any visitor unlikely; this one most of all. She had abandoned him once before. Why was she back?

Jessica.

Jessica was an ex-girlfriend. They hadn't parted on good terms. Something about him being too toxic. She went 'no contact' when she left. He had people keeping an eye on her social media posts. She was doing far too well for his liking. They hadn't spoken in over a year.

But there she was now, sitting across the Plexiglas, looking better than she had a right to.

He picked up the phone that served as their communications conduit.

"Did *they* make you do it?" she asked, "Did they make you push that man to his death?"

"I don't remember pushing him," Ichabod replied; he was aware he was being watched by the prison guards "This guy bumped into me; he started talking smack Next thing I know; I'm looking at his dumb ass dead at the bottom of a flight of stairs."

"Were *they* there?"

"*I don't remember,*" he repeated, this time with venom in his tone. He detested having to repeat himself.

"Have you seen any of *them* here?" she asked. The guards would have no idea what she was talking about.

"I only saw one of them here," he reported. "I haven't seen any of them since then." He examined her face. "Why are *you* here?"

"I saw your story on the news. I figured no one else would come and see you. And I know about the things you say you saw. Of course, only you saw them."

"*I saw them,*" he told her authoritatively. "You never saw them, because there's nothing special about you. You're a dried-up piece of toast."

Jessica didn't say anything in reply. She had learned not to say anything. *Think before you speak.* Is it true? Is it helpful? Inspiring? Necessary? Kind? She had run out of kind words for him a long time ago.

"They tormented me day and night," Ichabod Pob affirmed as he looked around, his peripheral vision still expecting to see *them* hiding in the fringes of his sight.

Except that there were none of them to see. That disturbed him as much as seeing them had. Where had they gone? Had even his demons forsaken him?

"You never said I was delusional," he recollected, looking at Jessica. "I'll give you that much."

"You would tell me that they would make noises, grab at you, and talk in your ear. That they moved your things and hid your belongings. Constantly."

"They gave me no peace." He paused. "You haven't asked how it is in here."

"It's jail. I'm pretty sure it sucks," she replied. "Anyway, you'll tell me what you want me to know. I remember how things are with you. I put fifty dollars in your inmate account, by the way. Not enough to make you rich, but enough that you'll have something to buy a candy bar with."

"I don't eat candy bars. They're junk. But you ate them. I saw your empty candy wrappers in the trash, thinking you were hiding your weakness from me. Nothing gets past me."

"I know that you don't eat candy bars. And I also know that you wouldn't push somebody down a flight of stairs, if you were anywhere near your right mind. You must have been in quite a rage."

"I should have you put on the jury," he scoffed.

"You'd still have to find eleven other fools."

"Are you going to visit again?"

"Probably."

"Why? To see how far I've fallen? Because I don't fall, and I don't break, sister."

"Unlike Melvin Broadshaw," Jessica noted. "He fell and he broke. He cracked up so bad that he died. And you don't even remember why you threw him down those stairs."

"You weren't there," he said. "You could have stopped me."

"I protected you against all sorts of things," she remembered. "But I can not protect you against yourself."

"My lawyer sent a shrink to evaluate me. I messed that introduction up. Maybe you could help me, for old time's sake?" He asked. He half-sobbed, a calculating ploy to secure her aid.

"I'll see what I can do to get you a re-introduction."

"For what it's worth, you did best of all of the people in my life," he told her. "I shouldn't have treated you so badly"

"Water under the bridge," she said. She recognized his manipulations now. Furious one moment, cajoling the next. *I love you. I'm leaving you. I love you. You're useless as tits on a bull. Who's my beautiful girl?* A carousel of lies.

She left, leaving him to whatever demons still considered him worth tormenting.

***

Jessica sat with Dr. Percival. The psychiatrist's private office was industrial yet comfortable. Brick walls and handmade quilts thrown over plush couches dominated the décor.

"I'm Dr. Hester Percival," the psychiatrist greeted. "I work for Mr. Pob's defense attorney, Ms. Lauermore. We're arguing that Mr. Pob lacked the requisite *mens rea* – mental state – to commit first degree murder in this case. The assistant district attorney wants to make a name for herself by getting a capital conviction, but Ms. Lauermore and I think we can argue down to a lesser charge. But Mr. Pob needs to cooperate with us. He said we had to include you. I don't know why. And, you don't have to help. He doesn't exactly elicit compassion. That volatile temper of his is more than a little off-putting. I simply introduced myself and he threw a fit."

"Did you call him Ichabod when you first met him?"

"Yes. That's his name, right?"

"Call him Robert or Mr. Pob. He hates the name Ichabod. His mother named him Ichabod because his father had died in an oil-well drilling accident while she was pregnant with Robert. Dad-to-be fell and broke his neck before Robert's birth. There's a story in the Bible about a woman who bore a son after the father died during the pregnancy. The Bible woman named the boy Ichabod. So, Robert's mother named her son Ichabod, too. The name means 'there is no glory.' Robert was bullied almost daily with Headless Horseman jokes. Kids can be assholes. To this day, calling him Ichabod can send him into a rage."

"He pushed a man down a staircase in a moment of rage," Hester noted. "Mr. Pob keeps saying that 'they' made him do it, that 'they' tormented him. That 'they' are to blame. Do you know what he is talking about?"

Jessica sat down in a comfortable chair. Dr. Percival's degrees hung on the wall. "Grambling State," Jessica noted.

"Class of 1977," Dr. Percival smiled, her brown eyes bright with the memories.

"You saw Doug Williams play football at college?"

"Yes, I did. Are you a college football fan?"

"I'm more into professional football. Robert used to like college football. Then he couldn't watch a game without throwing a shitfit," Jessica replied. "He started talking about seeing 'them.' He would have full-bore meltdowns. He said that he saw shadows move between him and the television screen and that the apparitions were purposefully obstructing his view. And that they caused him to knock over bowls of chips and spill his drinks on the carpet."

"So 'they' are his excuse for his abhorrent behavior? It's someone else's fault?"

"While I will agree that Robert takes near zero responsibility for anything – someone else is always too blame – I think he really saw 'them,'" Jessica replied. "Little shadow monsters that would come crawling towards him. Things that lurked in his peripheral vision. He said they would scratch at the window while he tried to sleep. That they would move things around so he couldn't find things."

"It sounds like a delusion, at best. A piss-poor excuse for his bad behavior at worst."

"He couldn't sleep, Doctor," Jessica explained. "He couldn't eat without getting upset. It messed up his entire being - body, mind, spirit. He got increasingly violent. Threatening. It was escalating. One night, while wielding a butcher knife and telling me that he was going to cut my throat, he told me to get out. I got out. Fast forward to now. He needs me now - he's given me his Power of Attorney, to take care of his affairs. I plan on going by his house tonight. To pick up the mail. Change the lighting. Keep it looking like someone is in residence."

"Why are you volunteering to help him?"

"Maybe the trauma bond is still there," Jessica sighed. "By the way, Robert wouldn't let me volunteer. He's paying me. Money helps him keep his distance from having to have any real relationships. I'll be 'in' with him as long as he is getting something out of me. Not a moment longer. He's made sure to tell me that I'm not worth the rib," she said, patting her lower ribcage.

"I got the ribcage lecture," Hester mentioned.

"Maybe that's it," Jessica smiled weakly. "The excised rib is morbidly curious as to the fate of the rest of the body. Regardless, I am here to help you and his attorney. You two ladies are in for quite the treat. I can make this a little easier for you. That's worth the effort right there."

***

Ichabod thought of Jessica's bright eyes as he lay on his cot. She had the same color eyes as him – a golden-brown that looked like the day's last sunlight on a hardwood floor.

Then he remembered *them*.

They had been around him every day and every night. Yet they hadn't followed him here, into his dark cell with no cellmate. Into the modern windowless dungeon. Their absence was a relief, notwithstanding his incarceration.

They hadn't swatted at his body, hidden his things, confused his speech, or incited rage in him for over forty-eight hours.

In the darkness of that underground windowless cell, he fell asleep. For the first time in decades, he felt oddly free.

***

It was nearing twilight Jessica entered Ichabod's house.

Jessica picked up his mail, accumulating in the entry mailbox. He had given her full authority to conduct his affairs. It wasn't a difficult assignment and Ichabod was paying her quite well.

She knew he would never actually thank her.

She tidied up the kitchen. His cell phone charger, the one he always complained about losing, was in the kitchen sink. She found two neckties hidden behind the couch while she was straightening up the house.

She remembered when they were together. He could never find the tie he wanted to wear. He was convinced someone had stolen them, or that someone else had misplaced the tie. *They* were moving his things. Except when he thought she was to blame. *"Where the Hell did you hide my red tie?"* he would scream out at her.

It didn't matter that she had no idea where the tie was located. Her lack of guilt was no defense.

Everybody he accused was always guilty in the Court of Ichabod Robert Pob. They all deserved terrible things for what they did to him. Melvin Broadshaw had learned that lesson harder than anyone else ever had.

Jessica put the charger on the breakfast bar countertop and placed clean dishes into the cupboards. Then she went back to her home, to a place he had never contaminated with his presence.

***

"It's a good thing I have you attending my business," Ichabod said. "They denied me bail. Otherwise I would be doing all this stuff for myself. They tell me that with my money I'm a flight risk."

"You seem more focused," Jessica noted, realizing he was bragging more about his financial liquidity than concentrating on his defense.

"*They* didn't follow me here," he told her. "Talking in my ear, hiding my things, grabbing me. That guy – Broadcaster or whoever – he talked smack to the wrong guy at the wrong time. I reacted automatically. Well, he asked for it: he got it. It was his doing."

Jessica elected to not point out the obvious fact that Melvin Broadshaw had not thrown himself down the stairs.

"Miss Lauermore, your attorney, is going to get the charges against you reduced," Jessica reported. "A diminished capacity argument."

"She's going to say that I'm crazy? *No effing way.* I'll do a whole stretch and keep my pride, rather than accept some sort of diminished capacity crap. I'm not crazy. I'm not stupid. Nobody is going to say anything otherwise. You just keep taking care of my business, while I'm inside. Even if that's the rest of my life."

Jessica didn't reply. Ichabod always knew better than everybody else. It made no sense to argue with him.

***

The night before trial, Ichabod Robert Pob could not sleep. He knew he had not done all he could to help himself.

Jessica had been his champion, even more than him.

Jessica. He was unexpectantly happy she was back in his life, even under these circumstances.

He found a part of him missing her terribly. Or at least missing her unconditional support.

That was as close to love as he was ever going to get.

It was an odd thing, he thought. *That I love her, now that I know I will never be with her.*

He looked at the bars to his cell.

It was *their* fault he was here. Not his. And even *they* had abandoned him now.

They had left; Jessica existed outside of his incarceration. The attorney and the psychologist would be gone soon, too.

He would have to find someone new to blame for his actions.

***

At trial, Ichabod Robert Pob was convicted.

Found guilty because he was guilty, Jessica thought to herself, as the jury foreman read out the jury's verdict.

She kept in touch with Ichabod afterwards. After all, he was still paying her.

He had asked her to sell the house for him. She could keep a portion of the proceeds as her fee.

The movers had emptied out Ichabod's house. Jessica had placed his furniture, clothing, and personal items in controlled climate storage. She cleaned the place up, readying it for a real estate agent to evaluate.

Jessica stood in the house, looking at the space on the carpet where his sofa had sat.

She remembered: back to when she had first seen *them*.

A shadow, in her peripheral vision, scampering across the floor. Looking for Robert.

Robert had been a bastard to her that morning. He had picked up a heavy Thanksgiving wreath, made of metal wire studded with sharp hard plastic decorations, and threatened to hit her with it. Delighting in telling her the damage the impact would do to her face. *After he was done with her face, no one would be able to even look at her again.*

As she had sat in shocked silence, the little shadow moved closer to him. It let her see it.

It circled him. Playing on the edge of his vision. Distracting him.

The crueler he got, the more of them appeared. They flew around him, dropped out of the ceiling on top of him. They were always in motion on the floors. Keeping him occupied with something other than hitting her.

Jessica liked *them*. *They* were her protectors.

"*Do you see them!?!*" he would cry out. "They're cutting off my air -- I can't breathe, Jess!"

"I don't see anything," she would reply serenely. But when he wasn't looking, she would thank them. Because every moment they tormented him was a moment that he was not tormenting her.

Then they warned her to get out. *They* knew something she didn't. She was already prepared to leave that night he came at her with the knife.

"You're right about one thing, Robert," she said as she thought about him sitting in his dark cell. "You were never crazy. *They* are real. I saw *them* all the time, too. And *they* loved me more than you did."

She watched the last little shadows escape out of the house, scurrying between the spaces in the walls. They had other assignments to attend to: they had others to protect.

"As for you, Robert," she whispered, watching the shadows leave. "The only monster you have left to face is the one that has always dwelled inside you."

That was as close to saying 'I love you' to the man who had tormented her as she could ever get.

Laura J. Campbell received the 2007 James Baker Award for short story for her tale "416175." She also was one of the five finalists in the Tales from the Moonlit Path's 2021 'Abandoned Places' contest. Over sixty of her short stories have been published in Chilling Crime Stories, Road Kill: Texas Horror by Texas Authors Volume 6, and other publications. Most of her recent novels and stories can be found on Amazon. When she is not writing, Laura can be found enjoying the other two 'R's': running and rock concerts. She is encouraged in her writing by her children, Alexander and Samantha.

The Mourner

by Johnathon Heart

Dianaimh mourned her brother by the sea. That blue-green mass from which he would never return. Her parents were silent. The rest of the village followed their unspoken doctrine. If the Chieftain and his wife called for no funeral and never wept, then neither would they. This left their daughter to carry the sorrow, looking into the brine and remembering. His hand on her hair when he returned from hunting trips, scuffling it until it was ruined. Her anger at this, even as she buried her gratitude at his attention. The grin on his face before he'd picked her up and put her on his shoulders. His smile at his wedding, focused on his bride. So many men saw a woman as an accessory, but Ian was in love.

She had told neither the widow nor her parents that she still heard his voice.

Mourn me, it whispered through the roars of the waves and their breaks on the shore. *Remember. Grieve.*

Rocky hills leading down to the coast shielded her from the village's eyes. So here she heeded its call, performing funerary rites alone. Her parents did not stop her, as to intercede meant to acknowledge the source of her grief.

This continued, day after day, until she heard the voice of another.

"Such a beautiful woman should not weep so."

A man stood in the tide, as beautiful as the waves and as savage. His red-brown beard trailed from his chin and his brilliant green eyes popped from behind it. Azure markings were painted over and under those eyes. His body seemed constructed of lean muscle, and he wore the kilt of a highlander, though she could not identify his clan.

"I weep for good cause," she choked out. "Leave me alone to it."

"Not until I have done everything I can to heal such tears," he stepped from the water, bare toes sinking into the sand. "Tell me how I may assist."

A bitter laugh was her response. "Are you a witch? Can you magick a dead man and his friends to life? Leave me."

At this, the man receded as the tide did. And as such did he return.

He spoke to her every day, disrupting the voice. As the waves' whispers begged for her sorrow, the man of the sea showed her its beauty. They walked together on the beach and spoke of things such as the patterns of shells and the moonlight upon the water. He introduced himself as Eich-Uisge, and she did not ask of his clan. It seemed wrong to do so. For moments, then minutes, then hours, she forgot to mourn.

In the churning waves, a dead voice cried rage.

One day, Eich-Uisge asked her the cause of her grief, and she answered. At the end of her story, a single tear rolled down from the handsome man's eye. She felt guilt, and resentment for the guilt. Not even here could her sadness be only her own.

Still she said, "I am sorry. I did not think you'd weep so readily for another."

"Do you not weep for another?" He wiped away his tear.

"I knew him well and loved him. What cause have you to cry like this?"

He stepped in front of her. "I mourn that you should know such loss. I would do whatever I could to free you from it."

And now he touched her hand—she did not stop him—and knelt to kiss the back of it. Another tear flowed from his eye, and her hand came up to wipe it away. This man on his knees conjured within her a vision of his beautiful face coming forward. In her mind, her fingers disappeared into his lips and prickled at the sensation of his tongue. These visions went on, murkier but more intense as they progressed. Desire surged and swept away all reason. Her legs weakened.

"Sweet stranger, who are you really?" she gasped.

"I am called The Kelpie, Lord of the Deeps. Do you fear me?"

"Not I." Yet deep within her she knew she should feel such fear, as she remembered this title from stories of drowning men.

"I have been afraid to tell you," said Eich-Uisge. "But long have I watched you from beneath the ocean. Your beauty, your sorrow, your bravery. You are my love, and the beating of your heart is like the throb of my pulse."

With this, her desire transformed to starving hunger. She'd felt unending grief too long, and now her body demanded pleasure. She pulled his lips to hers. In between their kisses, he offered again to ease her pain. Now, she told him exactly how.

Please grieve.

She forced the voice to silence.

He laid her down on the rocks by the shore. As his soft lips worked upon her, she looked out on the water. Watched it ebb and flow with her ecstasy. That kingdom he'd emerged from, which her brother had forever vanished to.

A horse with hair like grotesque seaweed. An eye emerging from beneath a moist dripping mane. Ian's voice calling out in wonder at the steed that swims as well as it runs. He jumps atop it and begs them to join him. They all follow.

That voice, now in more detail, with images as well as words. But Eich-Uisge pulled her away. He entered her, and moved in time with the tide.

The horse's back stretches, welcoming each new rider. They laugh at this with all the humor of grown men drunk enough to revert to boyhood. Ian looks back to see its tail is that of a serpent, that its hair has given way to the scales of a fish. But still he can only laugh at this strangeness. Even as the horse runs onto the beach, then onto the water beyond.

His power became intoxicating. He prompted her to forget even as she stared ahead into that ocean.

It is too late, when they realize that the horse does not mean to return. That their mount is slowly sinking. By the time their feet touch the water, they are too far out to swim back. Ian knows what it is and shouts. His friend Graham keeps laughing as the water rises to his knees. Anxiety breeds from danger coupled with the unfiltered joy of those who cannot see it. Some laughs turn to screams, but Graham cheers even as water reaches his chest.

Ian tries to climb off, hoping the tide will aid his now impossible swim back to shore. But his hands cling to the horse's back as if they are of one flesh. He is trapped. The mane ahead leads to upright ears. A neck extending and distending as it plows forward into the waves.

The voice begging for fear amplified. She stifled it and gave into joy.

He swallows wet salt. It burns. Bubbles rise from his throat and there is a freedom in it, not having to hold your breath after trying so long. Freedom exchanged for agony as the air your body thought promised does not arrive. Instead caustic fluid runs down into your lungs and your stomach and you are invaded by the sea. No matter how you move your neck the clog will not clear. Your final thoughts are incoherent fear. Around you are other squirming animals with air exiting their mouths. Some slow and stop before you. Others will struggle after you are gone.

You disappear dreaming of that light above. With one last remembrance of what it was to breathe.

His hand released her, and she rose sputtering but unafraid. The waves crashed. The mist blew across the shore. The water roared with his voice, and he pulled away from her.

She knew what he'd done, now. She did not run.

She rolled over, extended her arms, and took him into them. Like all men, he passed into unconsciousness at satiation. She looked up into the foggy sky, fingers trailing his collarbone.

There she found that silver necklace covered by his beard. She imagined the thick section just under the chin sliding into a horse's mouth and becoming a bridle. The bridle of a horse in the sea.

She allowed herself one childish moment of indulgence in a fantasy, in which she would go beneath the ocean and be Eich-Uisge's underwater queen. Then her grip on the necklace firmed. She pulled.

She ripped the silver bridle from his neck.

Eich-Uisge's eyes bulged. He gasped as his beard slid around his face and became a mane. As his snout lengthened and his hands and feet became hooves. He paced, shaking his hands until he fell forward onto what were now front legs. Soon he was a frustrated horse shaking its head and sputtering.

She grabbed his mane and whispered in his pointed ear, "Here's how you will help me."

He tried to shake her off, but she held firm.

She continued. "You will come back to my village. You will work our farms. You will help us harvest so much food that it could feed a hundred of the mouths that you killed. And then, in a year's time, I will decide what I do with you next."

The eye widened under the seaweed hair, terrified.

She felt the metallic weight at her side. "You have seen the knife under my skirt, or you are blind. I will ride atop you now, and if my hand sticks there, then this knife will slide in. Is that clear?"

The horse shook its head in something resembling a nod.

She jumped atop the kelpie, and rode it back to her village on its silver reins.

And as she went the voice of the sea rang out.

Yes. Avenge me.

***

The being that had once been *Eich-Uisge,* Lord of the Deeps, pulled an instrument across a field that it did not understand the purpose of. It did this every minute of every day. When it did not do it, it was whipped. There had been stubbornness, once, some residual haughtiness from when it had been a Lord. But it had learned that this would not serve it, here.

Some days, it saw the woman who had brought it here. At first it was furious. Then it forgot the reason for its fury as it forgot itself. Always she watched in return. Out of the corner of its eye it sometimes saw her lip quiver, her eyes moisten.

The plowing season came and went and still it was in the village, used as a communal horse in between long periods of time spent in a stable. When youths rode it, it imagined again sticking their hands to it and riding off in the briny depths. Why it had ever done this, it did not know. An instinct as primal as the one to feed or mate, but entirely disconnected from either of them.

Over the year, it withdrew from this desire as if from addiction. Then the guilt came.

Memories of empty faces once full of life drifting dead underwater took on new weight. When a youth rode it to the house of the maiden he courted and proposed there, it thought again of boys that age or younger begging to breathe. When it saw children playing in the mud, laughing at the condemnation of their parents, it thought of how it had once viewed disobedient children as easy targets.

Sometimes, it dreamed of a vast underwater palace. But only in the same way that all dream of life as Kings and Queens.

It woke from these dreams and cried into the night. It did not know why it did this.

One night, a hand touched it. A voice followed.

"Shh," it whispered. "You'll be fine. Fine."

Its empty eye saw *her,* the woman. It did not remember the source of her significance. Only warm feelings at her presence, combating pains of overwhelming hopelessness as myriad and natural as raindrops in a storm.

"I promise I will not extend this," her voice wavered. Her eyes moistened. The vague memory of a finger removing one of those beads of water. Why did this image hurt?

"You have suffered," she went on. "And still, my brother and his friends have not returned. I will not apologize, but there is no value in this."

But the being did not understand. Even as she came each night and stroked its neck and wept. Soon this misunderstanding replaced itself with warmth for the only woman who showed caring and inspired it in turn. When she came, the being expressed joy and rubbed up against her with its head.

For some reason, this made her weep harder, murmuring as she did, "I really loved you. Gods curse me for it, I did."

The year rolled on. By its end, the being was a plow horse, and Eich-Uisge no longer.

A day came when this plow horse lifted its head to find itself led by a rope through a forest of falling leaves. It remembered vaguely when those leaves had last fallen, when it had been something more.

This sparked a chain reaction of half-formed memories leading to thought. It recognized its own identity, and with that a mental sting it barely understood. An inarticulate awareness of the woman who pulled it along.

She led it through thin groves of trees, and intermittently across rocky plains. At one point it was pulled to the top of a hill, and looked over its edge to the ocean lapping at a distant shore. Another pang filled it.

At the core of the forest sat a circle of six standing stones. In their center sat an old white-bearded man.

"He has served his penance," the woman said.

The plow horse understood this. Something inside it awakened.

***

The voices from the sea whispered to Dianaimh, as they had. She closed herself off to them. She held the kelpie before Dall, the wise man.

"I see," said the old man. With effort, he pulled himself to his feet. "Now what do you wish for him?"

"I gave him my word," she said to him, to herself, to the voices. "So I will no longer hold him. I am a Chieftain's daughter and such oaths must be upheld."

Dall looked between the two of them. He then said, "Very well. You must give back the silver bridle that you once stole. Do not be alarmed by what ensues."

There would be no way to return from this. The voices of the sea dissolved into incoherent rage. But she would no longer maintain suffering.

She placed the bridle over the plow horse's neck. That neck began to thin, and its body shifted. Hands. Feet. Arms. Eich-Uisge was naked, and stumbled around the stone circle screaming and trying to cover himself. She restrained her pity, knowing that this was the kindest thing that she had done, even as he fell to his knees, head on the ground, and wept.

Animalistic noises transformed into human whimpers as the minutes passed.

"Ah yes," said the old man, after giving him his time to recover. "That is a penance served, if I've ever seen one."

"And now what?" Dianaimh asked.

"I must ask him," Dall approached the quivering form. "Lord of the sea, Eich-Uisge, you have been taught humility and made mortal. Now tell us: will you stay this way, or will you become kelpie once more?"

He only sobbed. The dam against her pity cracked. She placed her hand upon his back.

"It's over," she said.

He froze. His head turned up, his eyes wide. And now genuine tears streamed, not for another's fate, but for his own. Along with that, a recognition. She saw the same eye of the horse in the stable, suffering for reasons it could not understand.

"You are not a harsh enough judge, milady," Eich-Uisge whispered. "Your spirit is too warm."

"No," she wiped away his tears. "And of this, I am not ashamed."

Far away, the waves built and roared. They crashed against the cliffs, whispers of resentment cascading off from them. *Have you forgotten. Forgotten. Forgotten your brother?*

He had served his penance. No more was needed.

"He made you an offer, Eich-Uisge," she said. "Will you be mortal or Kelpie?"

His loving gaze turned her heart to a waterlogged brick.

"If I were a man, milady," she prayed he wouldn't say it. "Would you agree to be my wife?"

Hisses of a vengeful sea. Cries of *No! Never! The Dishonor!*

She examined his face for any sign of manipulation. But all she saw in those eyes was honest desperation. She wished that she did not return his feelings. Begged for the words to come easier than they did.

"I'm sorry, but you killed my brother."

"I understand." He stared at the grass beneath his feet. "Then I must decide what I shall do without your hand. Know that from the moment my eyes caught yours, I did love you. This was never a lie."

She turned away and into the trees. She could look at him no longer.

"Wise man, Dall," said the voice of Eich-Uisge, behind her. "I consider my options. But...to return to being a Kelpie means to return to the drowning of innocents, and I will not."

She ground her teeth as she listened. As the furious ghosts of the sea protested.

"I understand," the wise man said. "Know only that you have no home here."

"I will make one for myself, somehow. But I will not be a monster again."

She glanced back to see Dall smile, just before he spoke. "Then there is nothing more to be done, Eich-Uisge, for you are mortal already."

He nodded. "Thank you Wise Man."

He turned to leave, giving her one last nod, and paused on unsteady feet waiting for a goodbye. But she kept her eyes hard and warded off his words so that his mouth only opened for a moment before he turned away. He vanished into the forest.

Pain of the heart is weak vengeance, said a trickling of the tide. *Destroy him.*

At the moment that she could not see him, directionless pain surged, impossible to stifle. She charged. When she saw only his back, she slammed her palm against a tree for his attention. He turned. Her eyes locked onto his. Heavy breaths quivered through her.

"Perhaps," she recovered, into a smile. "I could lead you back to the village. And on the way there, we could discuss this proposal?"

Traitorous whore!

A silence. She almost wondered if he would not say yes.

But Eich-Uisge smiled as he took her hand. She forced a smile back, one begging for uncomplicated joy.

They traveled through forests and fields, over highlands and rivers, back toward where the thatched and smoking huts appeared, talking all the way.

Ignoring the ghosts inside her.

***

They were married by a priest who knew not what Eich-Uisge had been, surrounded by crowds of equal ignorance. Rumors circulated at the marriage of a Chieftain's daughter to an outlander, but she happily allowed it. If not her, it would be something else of interest.

They worked together by day, and she was moved by his genuine gentleness. Some days she wondered whether it had always been there, buried beneath a murderous intent. She wondered what their child would be, if nature so blessed them.

At night, Dianaimh cried out.

Often at the touch of Eich-Uisge. But even on the nights that he did not touch her, at the voices. More furious as time went on.

One night, she stepped onto that shore that had called for her mourning so long ago.

"I have done it!" she cried to the tides. "I have punished him, and he has learned! Now allow me joy, please!"

At first her only response was the unyielding roar of the waves. She was aware at once of the darkness. The fog in the sky covering the stars. The bright white of the foam was the only thing that made it partially visible. The sea pulled back, producing no waves.

Then a towering aquatic wall rolled across the beach, forcing her to jump away from it. And in its roar, they whispered.

We, the dead of the sea asked you to weep.

We did not set a terminus.

We demanded mourning; and we beg for more.

"I only mourn my brother!" she shouted. "Him, only!"

Other waves formed, and in each a plea.

And what of the unknown sailor the Kelpie drowned?

What of the children who were only called missing?

What of the maiden like you who swam out on a night like this?

Or the fisherman who could never feed his family?

And as it went on, images filled her of each of these deaths. She covered her eyes and still she saw them. So many riding the waterhorse. One mistake that they paid for eternally.

We are this and more, and we go unburied and ungrieved.

One woman's tears will never be enough.

But we will take every drop you give.

"No!" she screamed into her hands. "No more, I beg you."

Our need shall be sated.

And if not in your tears, then in his breath.

She shook her head. They were just voices and she was not afraid. But, with her eyes covered, she did not see the next wave. The water reached her ankle, and a *hand* grabbed and pulled. A chill ran up that leg to her chest as she understood: they had threatened to harm him. And *they could.*

She ran from that shore, and did not return to it.

The days and nights passed. They farmed and made love and were together.

But whenever he suggested going down to the sea, she would stop him. When he insisted, she fell to begging. At times she humiliated herself on her knees, weeping. Anything to convince him not to go.

"I don't understand, my wife," he'd say. "Why do you fear water so?"

She'd kiss him to distraction, and she'd take him to bed and mount him with desperate need borne only of the desire to feel close to him. To think of nothing else.

Until the day she felt her belly grow. Painful but welcome discomforts visited her. All at once she knew that what they'd sought had arrived. He kissed her belly every night. He made love to her tenderly so as to not disturb it. He whispered into her ear that both she, and that which awaited inside her, were his treasures. In the emotions brought on by her growth, she wept openly for joy.

The seasons came and went. Only some nights did she hear those voices. She drowned the seed of worry within herself. They had given up on her, and good that they had.

So the day came that she found herself ready. She whispered into Eich-Uisge's ear that a torrent had spilled from her, and laughed at his delayed understanding of her meaning. She knew that before the day ended she would feel great pain, but for now she would take her amusements where she could.

They held her down and led her through it as she screamed. At first she told herself that this torment was necessary for the future she dreamt of, but this alone did not get her through. She survived by finding him among them, holding his hand as the midwives did their work.

"It will be worth it, my love," he said. "It will be our child."

She kissed his hand as she had so long ago, and she pushed.

One of the midwives cursed. She looked up in a panic. "We're running out of water."

Another offered to go, but they shouted her down. The time was near. Not a single set of hands could be spared.

Eich-Uisge released her hand. "I will go."

To get water. Water from the river.

"No!" she shouted.

"Stay calm," one of the midwives held her. "Push."

"I will return soon, I promise," he smiled, and ran out. Ran for her.

"No!" she screamed, begging her body to not be here, not now, not in any state that would lead him to running for that river. "Please, no!"

"*Lay down! Push! Do not try to get up and control your stress! We are almost there!*"

She sobbed as she pushed. As she followed their instructions. She begged for it to not go as she imagined.

But as her baby emerged, the water never came.

***

She held baby Ian in her arms as she stared at the ceiling above. When they came in and told her, she did not react. It was only as she had expected.

Eich-Uisge, her husband, had been found drowned on the riverbank. They did not know how. They only knew that it seemed as though he had been pushed in. Many called it a murder, though any suspect had no motive. True, he had come to them an outlander, but in the year since none had been given cause to dislike him.

The baby wept openly. Not at anything that it could understand. At the sudden pain of life. At its own overwhelming first breaths, and from then on being in a world where it must breathe air, and not fluid.

What had she been? One woman. Against a thousand vengeful ghosts, once held at bay by the power of a Kelpie? Or by her grief for them? She did not know. They had come, and they had taken what they had wanted.

She rubbed Ian's small pink head with her finger, and gently squeezed the boy in her arms. She prayed that he would live, and breathe long. That she would not be alone.

Tomorrow, or the day after, whenever her body allowed it, she would scream at the rivers and the sea. She would demand him back without result, or at least curse them for taking him. She would pray for forgiveness for those deemed unforgivable, love for those deemed unlovable, knowing that the Earth and sky and especially the sea would treat it as hapless noise.

But for now, in this house in which she would raise a child alone, she mourned.

Johnathon Heart is the pseudonym of a prolific editor. Their horror pieces have been featured on the Nosleep Podcast, and are upcoming on the Thirteen Podcast and in Collage Macabre: An Anthology of Art Horror. Their fantasy/romance pieces are upcoming from Dark Rose Press and Grendel Press. They do not actually recommend falling in love with your brother's murderer.

Rumington Heights

by Jennifer Jeanne McArdle

Dearest Henry,

   Your wife is restless while you continue your geology research in the Arctic Station. If you thought I could spend two years waiting for you by the window, you married the wrong woman! (I DO miss you terribly and do hope you are keeping warm.)

I received a letter from one of my favorite students, Xiomara Villca, whom I taught in a Botany course at Pamera University. I mentioned her to you before but have never described her in detail. We have written to each other a few times a year since she graduated a decade ago. She invited me to see the work she has been doing with the farmers in her homeland as well as her experiments with horticulture and medicine.

Xiomara lives in the vampire holding called Rumington Heights.

You must now be terribly worried because I know how much you distrust the supernatural. But I have not made this journey without thought to the dangers. Do not get angry with me and please read further.

I am ashamed of how Xiomara and I became close. During one of my lectures, one of the other students mentioned a rare plant native to some vampire holdings.

"I pity those ignorant people living in holdings, taken advantage of by evil beasts," I said to my class. Xiomara, whom I had previously identified as one of my brightest students, seemed uncomfortable. "Is something wrong, Miss Villca?"

"Professor." She stood up. "I grew up in Rumington Heights, a vampire holding, and my family still lives there. Should I remind you that during the war, when refugees like my parents fled the war-torn areas, most people refused to offer us asylum. It was the vampire holdings that extended us that kindness. Without them, I would not be sitting in your class." She then gathered her things and left while the other students whispered about her. I ended class early and asked the registrar to give me Xiomara's dorm room number. Later that day, I knocked on her door, offering a rare cactus and expensive treats as an apology.

"Xiomara," I told her, "I truly apologize for my rudeness earlier today. You are a fine student, and if a young woman such as yourself could be raised in a vampire holding, then perhaps I need to rethink my opinions."

She let me into her room. As time passed, we grew close. As you know, I still feel that humans should be extremely skeptical in our interactions with the supernatural. However, I am a woman of science: Xiomara's claim that vampires can extend true kindness has always bothered me.

Do you remember that dolt, Gilbert Billeroy? That tall Professor of the Supernatural who always talks as though he has a cold? When that nosy fellow looked at the papers on my desk and saw the return address of one of Xiomara's letters, he started lecturing me:

"Rumington Heights was established six hundred fifty years ago by the Lord Rumington, who had been exiled from the largest vampire holding in Lexisburg. Rumington was a unique vampire: he was convinced that he could start a vampire holding where the majority of blood consumed by the resident vampires could be taken from herd animals and that humans would voluntarily join the holding without any forceful coercion or hypnotism. His holding is now a model for ethical vampire holdings everywhere."

Then he removed his silk handkerchief and blew his nose loudly! I eventually shooed Gilbert away, but I was reminded of what Xiomara had said. Xiomara has also sent numerous reports detailing the uniqueness of the soil in her homeland and the special properties of her herbs and vegetation grown there. I wonder if the changes in the soil are caused by the proximity to an open Hell Mouth (I suppose scholars of the supernatural call them Inter-Dimensional Portals, now, don't they?).

I cannot stop wondering why such a brilliant woman returned to live in such a cursed place. I hope to find either some great insight from her work there or to convince her to leave with me. Henry, please don't think me too foolish. I have ordered the carriage already (it was a bit expensive because most carriage companies avoid the place). I am set to depart next Tuesday and should arrive in Rumington Heights nine days later.

I know that you will likely receive a pile of letters every few months and not be able to respond timely. Still, I'd like to get out my thoughts in letters. And hopefully, you will be entertained by my tales.

With Love,
Margaret

***

Dearest Henry,

You'll be happy to hear that my journey to Rumington Heights only took eight days and was nearly incident free. I did not write you any letters whilst on the road because the rocking of the carriage afflicts me with dizziness, so every night, I fell asleep almost immediately after retiring to bed in roadside taverns. There were a few people making the journey with me, but nearly all of them, except one family, who are buying crates of apples grown in Rumington Heights, left our caravan before arriving in Rumington. The caravan has two hired bodyguards. Once we crossed the border into Rumington, they immediately advised that we put on necklaces of fragrant garlic. There hasn't been a reported incident of a vampire attempting to entice a traveler in nearly two hundred years, but one must always use caution.

One driver told me that some travelers actually refuse to wear the garlic because they have come to Rumington specifically to meet vampires. In response, I wore not only a garlic necklace but bracelets as well! However, I must remember my conviction, as a scientist: to always seek the truth!

I wondered if I might feel strange in an area surrounding a Hell Mouth, but I feel fine, if a little tired from the trip. Once we crossed the border, the land became quite steep and the rocks dark gray to jet-black in color. The trees come in three varieties: tall pines with reddish trunks and white and green needles, short grey trees with full blooms of electric green leaves, and mysterious willows that hang over the bodies of water. Even at high noon, a light fog seems to hang over the mountain peaks. I could just barely see the outlines of the castles and mansions that surround the villages where the humans dwell.

The villages are orderly, with well-kept roads and mostly uniform brick and stone houses displaying a few potted plants out front. Chickens wander the roads and all sorts of herd animals can be found in the villages' grazing lands, including all kinds of cattle, goats, sheep, asses, horses, pigs, and even alpacas. The children I passed were holding rabbits, pigeons, and guinea pigs. The villages aren't very different from most other mountain villages I've visited, except more organized and with more animals than usual.

Perhaps it is the mist, but everything seems just a bit quieter, as though every sound is happening under a soft blanket.

Despite my exhaustion, I arrived at the tavern owned by Xiomara's family. She still looks strong and youthful. I know that my hair has gone gray, and have many new wrinkles, but the sweet young woman told me I looked lovely.

"You see," she told me as we gathered my bags and walked towards her family's tavern, "there is nothing to be afraid of in a vampire holding. We could even leave your baggage there, and no one would think to touch it."

"Well! Let's not risk it."

During our walk, I saw many bees, butterflies, and even a tiny hummingbird. A healthy amount of pollinators is a good sign for the farmers here. The village is much more alive than I imagined.

"Your houses are all so well made." I got my first sight of the family tavern, a three-story building with large wooden doors.

"The council demands all buildings must be up to code and mostly uniform. Too many violations will get you evicted from the holding."

"Are there a lot of rules for living here?"

"Yes. Even vampires don't fully understand their natures. Keeping the harmony between us and them requires delicate balance—if we know a certain set-up and policy works, best not to change."

"Vampires might get more violent if the houses look too different?"

"No...maybe? We believe that order breeds more order. I'm sure Professor Gilbert could explain better." She smiled.

"You remember him?" I chuckled.

"How could I forget? Once he found out I was from a vampire holding, he was relentless with his questions! But his tests were easy, and he always brought interesting creatures to class, so most students liked him."

"Ah. Bribery. I guess compared to fairies in jars, plants aren't so interesting."

"Don't think that way, Professor. One of the things you taught me is that if humans learn to understand the *natural* world to the best of our abilities, the things we will be able to do will surpass the tricks of the supernatural."

"I'm glad all of my blabbering rubbed off on you!"

Henry, I know we were never blessed with children, but when I meet former students like Xiomara, I know that my legacy is secure. There is no greater joy than watching someone once under your mentorship flourish. Tonight, I will sleep in one of their spare rooms in the basement. The windows are locked as well as lined with fresh garlic.

With Love,

Margaret

***

Dearest Henry,

Your silly wife has made a fool of herself.

I slept well the first night in that basement room, but I awoke to the feeling of something tickling my nose. I thought that some daemon bloodsucker was tickling me, and I jumped out of my bed, screaming as I have never screamed before. What dropped from my face was but a large, black roach that skittered into the corner. Heaving, I was no longer afraid, just disgusted. I saw through my tiny window that the sun had already risen, so I decided to dress. I opened my bags and found so many more of the black bugs crawling inside.

That sight sent me howling as I dashed up the stairs and bumped into the maid. The milk she carried spilled all over my night clothes, but I pushed past her in my hysteria and ran outside to find Xiomara. I ran up garden steps and stumbled right into a bag of fertilizer. Your stupid wife! I started crying, and Xiomara came rushing to my side.

"Professor Alberry!" She spoke so delicately and softly. "Whatever happened to you? Let me help you get cleaned up."

I explained to her about the roach infestation.

She frowned and shook her head, her long braid swinging behind her.

"Professor Alberry, I am very sorry about the roaches. That is our most secure room for newcomers who have never lived near vampires so they are not afraid to sleep at night—but it hasn't been used in so long, I suppose the roaches moved in."

She helped me on my feet, and she called the maid, to whom I apologized (though I was a annoyed with her for not cleaning the roaches out of the room). I enjoyed a hot bath, and then I found Xiomara again.

"Our other rooms are occupied." Xiomara tapped her fingers on her table. "The agricultural techniques I've developed here have drawn visitors from other mountain villages that struggle with poor soil. They are here studying for a few weeks. We put some poison down for the roaches, but we can't promise that will kill all of them. You could…"

"I could…?"

"There is an extra day bed in my room. But…"

"My dear, I don't mind sleeping in your room as long as you don't mind sharing with a scared old lady." I forced a smile while still feeling quite ashamed.

"Anyone would be spooked by that many insects! I am ashamed of our lack of cleanliness! But you should know some things before you make your decision." She adjusted the red cap on her head and bit her bottom lip. I noticed her glance briefly towards one of the vampire castles, and a shiver went up my spine.

"I will have to explain later as I have promised to take our visitors around the farms," she continued as she motioned to the six men and women waiting outside the door of the tavern. "You are invited to come with us and share your tremendous knowledge. I've already told them that a Senior Professor of Botany from Ferdesberg University would be here today. They're quite excited to meet you. Would you mind moving this discussion until after we've returned from the fields?"

I agreed to Xiomara's request and joined her and the others. I asked them if they weren't a bit nervous, being in a vampire holding. Some of them said yes, but most shrugged.

"We haven't even seen one in the week we've been here," one woman told me. Others told me they were from vampire holdings themselves.

"We think because of the proximity to the Inter-Dimensional Portals, the soil here and back home is pretty similar."

"Why do you call them Inter-Dimensional Portals now?" I asked. I know we like to joke that scholars of the supernatural are constantly creating increasingly technical terms for horrible things, but I wanted to understand their reasoning. A tall young man with a pale complexion turned to me.

"We know that vampires can't travel too far from them without great suffering and eventually dying. And if a human looks into them, the images they see are horrific—some men have been driven to insanity. But is it really 'hell'? Have you heard of the tribe of people who live near the multi-colored volcanic lakes? In the past, the locals used to believe that the souls of the dead went to one of the lakes after bodily death. But modern scientists tell us that the lakes are strange colors because of the minerals in the water. We have no real proof that damned human souls exist behind those portals. Perhaps, too, vampirism is just a different way to be human."

I accepted this young man's somewhat reasonable explanation without argument, and we continued our observations. Xiomara pointed out the names and varieties of different crops and detailed her agricultural planning.

"Remember to rotate your crops annually. Leafy vegetables, like cabbage, should be planted in corn fields after the corn is harvested to replenish the soil."

She pointed out a row of herbs she claimed kept local bugs and pests from the soil. We came to a patch of tomatoes. Xiomara knelt to look at them more closely. Suddenly she ripped a whole plant up from the roots, spots of black dirt flying everywhere.

A foul smell reminiscent of human pus immediately smacked me in the face. I gasped, covered my mouth, and looked at the plant. Its roots were covered in a purple-gray slime.

"It's diseased and will have to be burned," Xiomara said while covering her own mouth.

"How did you know?" asked one of the shocked farmers. "This same disease killed a quarter of our crops last year, but we had no idea the plants were sick until they were already dead."

"Look very closely at the stem and you'll see some tiny black, swirled lines."

As I predicted years ago, Xiomara has developed into quite the brilliant horticulturalist. While her work here is important, I can't help but wonder how many more people she could influence if she moved to a large university and was able to spread her knowledge more widely.

Anyway, Henry, you must be wondering about what Xiomara told me about our sleeping arrangements. After we returned to her family's tavern and the other visitors went about their day, Xiomara told me that we should talk before the sun went down and took me to her personal gardens. I followed behind her as she checked the leaves of a few of her plants and then led me to a couple of stone benches.

"I want you to know that if you sleep in my room, we may be visited by a vampire at night," she said abruptly after staring at the ground for a few moments.

"What? Why? Is it dangerous?" I wrapped my arms around my body and looked out towards the castles in the distance.

"Probably not." She sighed very deeply before continuing. "Do you know that before I went to university, I hardly ever saw a vampire here?"

"That sounds very lucky. What changed?"

"Unless we are important people, or we do direct business with or for them, the vampires usually do not care about us. With some exceptions, they aren't allowed to drink our blood. The vampires feed, taking a little blood from each type of herd animal. If a vampire drank only the blood of cattle or dog, he might get sick and crave the blood of humans more than ever. But by drinking a mix of blood from many species, the animals can survive, and the vampire also survives and does not need the blood of humans.

"It is a good system. The vampires protect us. For hundreds of years, people who have been persecuted for their religion, race, their sexual urges, or whatever else, have come to vampire holdings and found acceptance, like my own parents escaping from war, as long as they adopt the rules and lifestyle of the holding."

"It shouldn't be only vampires that accept people in need. We humans should try to do better."

She shrugged. "I have known since I was a child that our diets were too heavy in meat and lacking nutrition because the poor quality of soil here. When I returned from university, I wanted to work with the local farmers to grow better crops and improve our diets. One young farmer, Alexander, was really enthusiastic about my work and helped with my experiments although he had no formal scientific training. I grew close to, Alexander—we even talked about marriage. My parents were happy. They have been afraid since I left for university that I might settle somewhere far away."

"Oh." I knew that Xiomara had never married. Before, I had assumed that she simply had no interest. But this detail made me worry. Where was Alexander now?

"But you can't change anything without getting approval from the Council first. The Council consists of the most important and wealthiest humans and all of the active vampires. The catatonic ones, such as Lord Rumington himself, are only awakened for special occasions. Eventually the Council agreed to let me make my case for changing how we farmed. I came ready with a very detailed presentation. Walking into the Great Hall and having all forty-five of them stare at me was plenty intimidating. Younger vampires look mostly human, except their complexion is ashen. Their teeth are sharp, their fingers long, and their eyes have a slight unnatural glow. And yet, something about them is so attractive that you want to stare. You should not look directly into the gaze of a vampire, mind you. The older vampires look stranger—their limbs are longer, their bodies are thinner, and their faces stretched. Still, they have a beauty that is hard to explain."

Xiomara stopped talking and adjusted her cap. I saw her glance up at that castle again.

"There was one vampire…" Her voice trailed. "Sorry. I get nervous speaking his name, but it is light out. Lord Clifford Harrington. He asked me a question, seemingly very intrigued by my work. I did not look directly at him, but he continued to ask questions and offered great insight. I could tell that he was paying more attention to me than I think nearly anyone ever has. Still, I remembered how everyone had always warned me. After the meeting was over, I was talking to Alexander's father. I saw his expression briefly change to one of anger, but then he hid it. Someone tapped my shoulder, and I turned to look directly at Lord Harrington."

"Oh dear." I felt my heart race. Xiomara stared at the ground for a few moments. "What happens when you do that?"

"Sometimes nothing. But vampires have to look at you directly to start hypnotizing you. I should have looked away immediately—but I didn't. It's true that once a vampire uses their hypnotism, the feeling is addictive. However, I think part of you needs to *want* the hypnotism for it to work. Your guard must be slightly lowered…and I can't lie: part of me was curious about this strikingly intelligent figure with his deep, smooth voice. You must understand. After I went to university, I learned so much from all my professors. I love my village, but to be able to talk about science again--that was a blessing. 'Blessing' is the wrong word."

"So? Didn't you say that vampires in this holding aren't allowed to drink human blood?"

"As I said, there are some exceptions. Lord Rumington developed a potion that he gives to all vampires that join this holding. It makes vampires unable to drink blood from a victim who resists them. Actually, they can drink the blood, but it slowly poisons them and gives them excruciating pain. Vampires here must even calm the animals before they drink from them."

"Then, there should be nothing to fear?"

"Yes, but, for a period of about eight months, I willingly let Lord Clifford drink my blood. Not anymore, but sometimes he visits me in the night to watch me sleep even though I will not let him drink."

"I don't understand." My whole body trembled with fear at the thought of some vampire drinking Xiomara's blood. Or my blood.

"The sun is setting, so I will explain more later. I have become more fearless at night and sleep with the window open. But I still cover all my skin and adorn my room and bed with garlic. I suggest you also cover yourself and sleep with garlic as well, more for your own peace of mind than because of any real danger. As long as you don't start talking to him, there is no way for him to hypnotize you, and if you resist, drinking your blood is not worth the pain he would experience. If you hear him in my room, try not to look directly at his gaze. He rarely comes anymore."

Henry, do you know how foolish your wife is? I was absolutely horrified and disgusted at Xiomara's story. But I also wanted to know why she had let him drink from her. How can one say they went to a vampire holding but never actually saw a vampire? I realized this would be a low risk way to see a vampire, if he came in the night to watch her sleep. Are they just another part of nature we don't understand?

I agreed to sleep in her room. Would a love sick vampire be more disturbing than hundreds of roaches? Anyway, my hand pains me now. Oh, Henry. Don't scold me too much when you see me again.

With Love,
Margaret

***

Dearest Henry,

For the last three nights, I have slept in Xiomara's room. I have covered myself and worn garlic. If the vampire has come, I haven't seen him. We have spent our days climbing up and down to the fields, checking on the plants, so I have been utterly exhausted by the time we retire. Xiomara's parents are excellent cooks and make wonderful, fragrant dishes. I wake up to the sounds of beautiful birds chirping, the air is invigorating and clear, my left knee hasn't bothered me, and there is no sense of urgency here. I can understand more why some people might choose this life.

This morning, Xiomara let me know that she had a slightly different plan for us today. She took me back to her private gardens again and let me examine the different plants she is growing.

"This is quite the odd mix you have here," I commented.

"It is, indeed." A bright smile beamed from her broad, tan face and her narrow eyes crinkled.

"And it might be my most important work. Come down the stairs to my basement. I am sorry if

you see any roaches."

Not without a little fear, I followed Xiomara down the steps, and she took me past the room where I had stayed to a different room. There were stone tools for grinding plants on the tables and multicolored bottles of different herbal medicines as well as several pots, a fireplace that needed to be cleaned of its ashes, and a few portable gasoline burners.

"I should give you some background before I explain my work. Each vampire here is allowed to keep up to four human thralls."

"A thrall?" I asked. Xiomara played with a stray thread from her dress for a few seconds before explaining further.

"Thralls let vampires drink their blood. Thralls are addicted to their vampire masters as much as the vampire is addicted to the thrall's blood. Some thralls live for weeks, months, or years, slowly wasting away after gradually losing blood and health. The vampire is usually upset after losing his thrall, but he cannot control his addiction, either."

"So…you were a thrall of that Lord Clifford? But you are healthy now. You aren't wasting away, are you?"

"With great willpower and suffering, it is possible to naturally break that addiction." She gave me a determined look before turning to her bottles again. "But most people cannot. So I am developing medicine to reduce their suffering. This encourages their bodies to produce more blood to make up for blood they lose as well as replaces some lost nutrients. It helps them live longer. But it's not a permanent solution."

"Have you tried to make a drug that would break the addiction?"

"You know me well. Of course I have, but let's not talk publicly of that. I do not want to get people's hopes up. It would require much more funding. I don't have the money to buy all the exotic plants I would need. Later, I will let you go through my notes as long as you keep their contents to yourself and only read them down here. But I have appointments to make."

Xiomara gathered up some bottles into a pouch and informed me that we were going to visit the mansion of one of the vampires and his thralls, if I would come with her. I agreed. She gave me a necklace of garlic just in case, but the vampires would not be awake during the day. We walked for about forty minutes past the quiet homes. I had a fleeting sense of dread when I noticed that as we approached the mansion, the animals seemed just slightly more alert than usual.

We arrived at the mansion of Lord Donelli, one of the younger vampires. Xiomara told me that each vampire had his or her own style. Donelli's home had a classic look, with large white columns, wide windows, and plenty of hanging, vine-like plants.

"This holding requires that the vampire master care for his thralls and their families. They have the nicest homes, or whole rooms or wings in the vampire's mansion. Their family also gets a significant allowance before and after the thrall's death. The four thralls of Donelli and their immediate family live in different wings of this mansion."

A young woman greeted us at the door. Xiomara told me she was the younger sister of one of the thralls. The rooms of the mansion contained polished marble floors and walls, pure white human statues, large paintings of famous battles, red velvet curtains, and large oriental rugs.

"So having a willing thrall is the only way they can drink human blood?"

"Yes. They can survive on just animal blood. But the urge to drink from humans never fully goes away."

The sister led us down a long hallway and opened the door into a bright, airy room. In the center, on a wide couch, a languid young woman with long, blonde hair, a pale complexion, and wistful eyes was stretched out. She had not bothered to dress herself this morning and wore her white, lacy nightclothes that exposed delicate shoulders and part of her bosom. Two deep red scabs pulsed on the left side of her neck.

"My sister has been looking forward to your arrival," said our young guide. "Her lethargy has been increasing this past week."

"Isabella." Xiomara stepped towards the sickly woman. "Sit up, dear. I have your medicine."

Isabella drank greedily from Xiomara's bottle, and then dramatically dropped herself backward and let the bottle fall out of her hands to the floor. Xiomara picked her bottle up without so much of a sigh of complaint. Isabella caught me rolling my eyes.

"Who is this?" She suddenly sat up with more energy.

"This is Professor Alberry. She taught me while I was at university." Xiomara put her bottle in her bag and smoothed her dress.

"She's come to gawk at us vampire loving freaks?"

"No, no. I've invited her to come. She's helping me with the farmers. She's one of the best in her field. We should all be honored by her visit," Xiomara spoke before I could respond.

"What mortal human could have more knowledge than an immortal vampire? You should go back to working with *Lord* Harrington on your plant experiments rather than some old kitchen witch with a fancy title."

Xiomara looked angry for a few seconds, but then she smoothed her expression. "I should get Liana her medicine. She must be feeling terribly ill as Donelli drinks from her more than from you."

Both sisters shot us evil looks as we exited the room. Visiting the other thralls was less eventful; they were actually sicklier than the dramatic Isabella. Just looking at them made me feel exhausted. We returned home in time for lunch.

"So, what happened with this Lord Harrington? How did you break your addiction?" I asked her.

Xiomara sighed deeply and drank some water. "First he visited me in my home at night, and we spoke only of science. He did not drink from me. I kept the relationship a secret, but I thought that I could control how far it went. But eventually…he did what vampires do, and he began to drink. My family, my parents, my brother and his wife, found out and received a large allowance and gifts. Alexander was heartbroken. Cliff—Lord Harrington--moved just me to his castle. He tried so hard to please me. He bought me nearly anything I asked for. I yearned to be around him, but each time he drank, it hurt. And I became too weak to do my work."

"God in heaven!" I looked up at the sky. "How did you survive?"

"It is not easy to break an addiction to a vampire. But most vampires choose thralls who lack ambition because it is easier to keep them. You saw Isabella. Even before she became a thrall, she was lazy. I went home a few nights a week to do my work, which made Clifford nervous. However, he allowed me some nights away from him because he feared for my health and encouraged my work.

"One night, Alexander came to my house. He embraced me, and my passion for him returned at once. I decided then that I could not return to the castle. That night, I wrapped my neck with cloth, covered my whole body in garlic, and tried to sleep. Of course, Lord Harrington came knocking on the window. I did not answer. I thought I would explode with the desire to get up and let him in. I sweated so much that my bed was soaked the next morning. The next night, I asked my mother to tie my arms to the bed before I slept. This continued for a couple of months until the addiction subsided, and I could sleep without tying myself down. I saw Alexander only during the day and went on with my work."

"Weren't you afraid someone would tell the vampire about you and Alexander?"

"I was. But I loved Alexander. And I guessed that Lord Harrington really did love me in his own way and would learn to accept my decision. He had other thralls. But you are right to worry about Alexander's fate." Xiomara swallowed and struggled to hold back tears. I rubbed her back. She wiped her eyes with the back of her hand.

"He was found murdered one night, his throat slashed and his limbs broken and twisted. His body was hung up on a pole."

"Oh, God." I breathed out.

She shook her head. "That was a few years ago. Lord Harrington still enters my room and watches me sleep. But he has never tried to drink from me--nor will he. To drink the blood of an ex-thrall is deadly for vampires. Also, his blood addiction to me is gone."

"How can you be sure?"

"He may visit me, but my family no longer gets his allowance." Xiomara sighed again looked away. "My brother and his wife still have the gall to complain to my parents even still, even after…" Her cheeks puffed, and she squeezed her fists.

"Then why does he come?"

"His physical addiction is gone, but his emotional one is not."

"Do you think you will ever be able to marry?"

"Who knows? Maybe Lord Harrington will grow bored of me. What potential husband wouldn't be nervous to romance me? But I am considered an old maid now, aren't I? I'd imagine that even if I left Rumington Heights, find a husbanding a husband would be difficult."

"You dare call yourself old in front of a woman whose hair has turned completely gray?" I rolled my eyes. Xiomara giggled, and we did not talk of vampires or dead fiancés for the rest of the day.

Missing you dearly,

Your Margaret

***

Dearest Henry,

The moment I have been dreading finally came last night. I woke in the middle of the night to the sound of a great thud. Without thinking, I jolted up. My senses came to me before I could remove my blindfold or my ear buds. I immediately hid myself back under the covers. But Xiomara's family's tavern is quite old, and I could feel just the slightest vibrations of footsteps. I tried to slow my heartbeat and my breath as I pulled the covers over my face. Then, I pushed the blindfold up and tried to peek under the blanket towards the window and Xiomara's bed.

I could see the figure of a tall, thin man. The moonlight behind him made him look as though he were glowing, from the top of his blonde head to the bottom of his expensive black shoes. His clothing was well made but would have been fashionable a hundred years ago with its extra lace—he looked a bit feminine by today's standards. Still, I could see by his broad shoulders and thick legs that he must have been quite the athlete when he was still a normal man. He stood over Xiomara, who had not woken from her slumber, and watched her chest move up and down.

He slid the claw at the end of his long pointer finger from the top of her head, down her forehead, over her chest, her stomach, her legs, and to the end of her toes. He leaned close to her face and breathed in deeply, getting her smell.

Why was he so obsessed with her? I wondered, clenching all my muscles in fear. Was he her ancestor (I imagine incest isn't unheard of for awful vampires). But he was blonde, tall, pale, and angular, while Xiomara was short, stocky, brown, and with broad features, and as she said, her parents had come from far away.

Without thinking, I let out a low squeak. My whole body froze, I clenched my eyes shut, and I heard the burst of his jump from his former position to the thud of his landing next to my bed. He began to speak lowly, but his words were muffled by my ear plugs. As Xiomara said, his voice was very deep and smooth. Tears welled up in my eyes as cold air was breathed onto my face. Then came a light touch, as light as roach legs, on my neck as he pulled the blankets from my face. His fingers stopped a couple of inches from the necklace of garlic.

"Ah, sweet, granny professor," his face must have been very close because even with the ear plugs, I could understand him. "I am lucky I have not eaten in a few days or the smell of your garlic might make me retch. Why don't you look at me? I know you are a professor. The other night I visited while you slept and looked through your papers and your bags. I've seen your letter to you husband. You must be curious to look. Don't you want to give Henry an accurate description of my terrifying visage?"

I tried to clench my jaw tighter, but instead a sob burst from me and tears leaked down my face.

"Hmph. I suppose it's just as well you don't. You're much weaker than your student. I've never been attracted to weak humans."

I felt something wet and cold on my ears, and I had to hold back a gag as I realized he was licking me.

"Too bad. Your blood would taste of outside things and faraway places."

I heard another thud, the squeaking of the window's hinges, and then I could hear the crickets chirping again, and the room became warmer. Even still, I did not dare move for what felt like hours, but I suppose I must have fallen asleep because when I finally opened my eyes next, I could see sunlight coming seeping through my blindfold.

Perhaps I should depart from Rumington Heights. I am not sure, Henry, if this old lady's heart could take another encounter like that again.

With Love,

Margaret

***

Dearest Henry,

After I wrote to you, Xiomara woke up. She brewed me tea that calmed my nerves.

"I know this is frightening, but he is playing with you. He will not drink your blood. It is not worth the pain," she reminded me. And Henry, you might think I am foolish, but should I be scared by some craven, monstrous peacock? I am resolved to stay and finish the last few weeks of my planned trip.

Xiomara tells me that there will be a Council meeting in a week's time. She plans to attend to plead her case for more funding for her medicines. I will join her presentation as an expert consultant. We have been working hard on the materials and on refining some of her medicines for the thralls.

I hope my prattling stories are entertaining you. But knowing you, you're happy looking at your rocks.

With Love,

Margaret

***

Dearest Henry,

The Council meeting was this afternoon in the Great Hall in the center of the cluster of villages in Rumington Heights. The building is tremendous, resembling in style old churches because of its stone carvings of strange gargoyles. The inside is all dark stone and wide columns and in the front of the room is a large stage. All forty-five of the vampires were seated there by the time we arrived. From far away there is no danger in looking directly at them. They dressed in clothing from older time periods. The twelve female vampires present were more fashionable than the men, sporting elaborate hairstyles and great, gaudy hats that sparkled in the moonlight shining through the high windows. Some of the vampires had extremely long arms and large ears and long faces, their eyes glowing, while others looked more human. Xiomara told me that vampires older than four hundred years are sleeping in a catatonic state. Seated next to the vampires was a group of about twenty well-dressed humans.

I must admit: after I got over the shock of seeing the vampires, the Council meeting was actually quite dull. The Council resolved disputes between neighbors, mostly about land use and zoning. I was nearly falling asleep in my chair until I hear a familiar voice ring out through the hall.

"Finally the Council would like to address the request of one, Ms. Xiomara Villca, and her professor, Margaret Alberry." It was Lord Harrington's voice. I shivered and gripped Xiomara's forearm. She did not seem fazed and took my hand in her gloved hand and adjusted her scarf as she picked up her presentation materials and brought them to a table placed in front of the Council. We spoke, looking mostly at the humans and avoiding the gaze of the vampires. We made her case for more funding and detailed how we would spend the money and answered a few questions. We were nearly done till I heard someone shout from the corner of the stage. Without thinking, I turned to look at the source, but luckily, he was not looking at me.

"Wait," came the gentle voice of a vampire who looked nearly human and was dressed in modern garb. He would eternally be a young man with soft, sweet features.

"I heard a rumor that you might be able to develop a medicine that actually breaks the addiction between vampire and thrall. Is it true? And would it be only for the thrall, or the vampire, too?" His voice was shaking. I caught Lord Harrington glaring at the young vampire.

"I, well…" Xiomara adjusted her cap. I gripped her hand to help her with her composure while wondering why she was so shocked by this question. She steadied herself. "That may be a possibility in the future. And if I developed any medicine capable of breaking addiction, I would take great care to make it available for both vampire and thrall."

"The temptation to drink human blood is so strong." A stray string of drool leaked from his mouth. "Wouldn't it be better if we could drink just a little and not create an addiction?"

There was murmuring amongst the Council and the crowd as well.

"Order, order." Lord Harrington's voice rang through the Great Hall. "Let it be known that the Council will deliberate only on the funding for the medicines requested in Ms. Villca's official paperwork. If you, Ms. Villca, wish to discuss funding for future, other medicines, you will have to plead your case to the Council at a later date. You will be notified within a few days regarding your proposal."

"Thank you for your time and generosity," Xiomara spoke with no emotion, and we back down.

"Who was that young vampire who spoke?" I asked Xiomara the next morning.

"He is Balthazar Genativi, the youngest vampire here, only changed about five years ago. One of the vampires who had been living here for a few centuries began to get too rough with the animals and started harassing women at night. The Council voted to hang him outside the range of the Hell Mouth until he died, leaving a spot open for a new vampire. The brother of a beloved thrall of one of the senior vampires had been dying of tuberculosis. She convinced him to change her brother into a vampire. But he did so without approval from the Council, so his transformation remains a bit of a scandal."

Henry, the more I learn about vampire holdings, the more I feel that there are so many things going on that I'd never hope to understand.

With Love,
Margaret

***

Dearest Henry,

I have decided to end my trip early. I have already packed my things and am awaiting a carriage.

A few days after the Council meeting, news reached the tavern that the young Lord Balthazar had a wooden stake stabbed into heart and was hanged near the Great Hall. That afternoon, Xiomara ripped her plants up and putting them in a great pile before tossing some oil on them and setting them aflame.

"What are you doing?" I shouted when I saw her.

"It's not safe for me to continue my work at this time." Her voice croaked. "Those who killed Balthazar wanted to send a message. If they think I am actually close to developing a concoction that will break the blood addiction, they may come after me. But no matter. I will keep my notes locked away. Perhaps if things change, I will be able to continue my work again."

"But what about all the thralls that rely on you for medicine?"

"They will have to live without for the time being. We all will suffer from Balthazar's foolishness."

"Your people suffer much because of those evil hell creatures! They would even kill one of their own just for suggesting that things might change."

Xiomara turned to me as the flame danced over her pile of herbs, hundreds of smells filling our nostrils. A smile that didn't reach her eyes spread across her face. We both watched a handsome rooster with a shiny black tail pick at some grains.

"I often wonder, if our animals could choose, would they want to stay domesticated and let us coddle them and help them propagate for eternity although we eat and cage them? Sometimes they hate, chase, and murder their own kind, even their own brothers, to protect their lives with us."

"Yes?" I wasn't sure why she was suddenly talking about animals.

Later, Xiomara asked me to have breakfast with her on one of the highest cliffs in in Rumington Heights the next morning. By then, I had already told her that I would leave on the soonest carriage out of the area. She agreed. Even so, she insisted I see the sunrise.

We woke up before dawn and still wore garlic as we climbed for about forty minutes without speaking. I kept thinking about everything that had happened as a breeze carrying strong scents of wildflowers and weak scents from the distant villages and animal herds caused our scarves to wave behind us. By the time we reached the spot where Xiomara wanted to eat, the sun had risen, and we shed our extra clothes and garlic. Suddenly, I realized what Xiomara had been trying to tell me, and my blood felt cold in my veins.

"You don't hate Lord Harrington because he didn't kill Alexander."

She shook her head. We looked down at the valley where we could see the tiny specs of animals grazing. "My brother's family could not break their addiction to Lord Harrington's money. They thought I would return to him, if Alexander was gone."

"I could get you a job at the university. You could leave this wretched place. They don't deserve your brilliant mind."

"No," she answered firmly. "The people here were rejected by the rest of the world. They need this village and its safety. I would be a freak in your world. Here, I have respect and power, even if it makes people fear me. Even if they try to ruin me, I will continue my work."

I watched the sun come up, watched the light beams reflect through the mist and off the black, jagged rocks, and the dew on the long, green grass. The sky was a soft purple this morning, and some small birds sang some sweet, long notes. Rumington Heights does have its charms, Henry, but I doubt I'll ever visit again.

With Love,
Margaret

Jennifer Jeanne McArdle lives in New York State with her partner and an agent of chaos (her dog). She works in animal conservation, but previously she's taught ESL in Korea and Indonesia and also worked with nonprofits in Asia and the US. More info on her website:

https://jenniferjeannemcardle.blogspot.com/

Twin Temptation
by Barend Nieuwstraten III

A ndred roused to a noise in the dark. His eyes darted about in the blackness of night, seeing nothing in the sea of shadow that surrounded him. A light sleeper, he was not unaccustomed to waking in the middle of the night at the slightest disturbance. The hoot of an owl, the barking of dogs, even the scuffing of guard's boots outside his door as they adjusted stances in their long watch. But every time he had, there had been some faint trace of light. If not from the moons and stars outside his window, at least the orange glow beneath his door from candles in the corridor. But there was nothing. To achieve this, his curtains would need to be drawn and some long garment, rug, or pelt dragged across the crack under his bedroom door. An absent-minded servant might have drawn the curtains shut by mistake, but to obscure the light beneath his door meant someone had to be *in* the room. For he certainly did not recall pulling himself out of bed, crawling along the floor to drag his crippled body across the stonework to plunge himself into darkness before making an unassisted climb back into his high bed.

Abandoning reliance on his eyes, he listened. If someone was in his room, having made sufficient noise to wake him, they certainly weren't making any noise now. Whomever was hiding in the dark, saw far better in it than he, if they knew he was awake at all. He contemplated calling for a guard, instinct demanded it of him, but something about this situation gave him pause to reconsider. If someone was here to assassinate him, there'd be no real need to block the light from under the door. An excessive precaution that would take time better spent slitting his throat or pouring poison down it as he slept. Something far more intriguing was at play. He half smiled, curious.

After hearing a subtle creak of leather, a spark flashed beyond the foot of his bed. It lit a small portion of the room for the briefest of moments, but he'd not been looking in that direction. Now his eyes were trained there as he anticipated another. It came again, revealing a hint of four hands, then again, adding a candle holder, candle, and flint. Soon a lit wick birthed a baby flame that grew into candlelight. There, at the foot of his bed, two feminine figures stood in elegantly crafted layered, leather armour. As the light grew about their hips, first and foremost, Andred noticed each carrying a pair of curved eleven shortswords upon their belts. From descriptions he'd heard, these were not allies stood before him. Yet, he still lived.

"Good morning," he quietly said, as two slender women appeared before him.

"Morning," they both said, as they each moved around different sides of his bed in a sultry pincer movement. They moved with such gliding grace that it seemed their feet only touched the ground by choice. The one on his left placed the thick candle and its iron holder on his bedside table before the other pointed to the edge of his bed. "May we?" she asked.

He nodded, curious. They both sat on either edge of his bed and twisting to face him. Their long, elegant faces were beautiful to behold. The cool colours of their eyes seemed to glow in the candlelight. Pale of complexion and fair of hair, their features were too noble to be purely of human blood. Half elven and barely distinguishable from each other. Further confirming his suspicion, he knew them by reputation only.

"Princesses Avkiyara and Astryksia Aeligis, I presume," he said, having been forced to master their unusual Ijcari names. Their mother being a frost elf from the frozen wastes of the cold continent beyond the Southern Sea. Their father, King Garaug Aeligis of the neighbouring kingdom, Southmarch, east of Andred's own. They were figures of interest in the dealings between their two kingdoms.

"Greetings Prince Andred, fourth to bear the name, of House Belethon, rulers of the kingdom of Cliffguard." one of them said.

"A great deal of formality to be uttered by one already seated upon my bed," the forty-year-old prince said. They were a decade older than him, yet the pair looked half his age.

"Well," the other said. "This is the first time we are meeting and there are no heralds present to observe the proper protocols. So, some curtesy must be undertaken ourselves."

The prince pressed his hands down onto his bed, straightening his arms, to push himself up against his bed head. One of the princesses pulled him forward, while the other bunched pillows behind him. Despite their battle-ready appearance, they smelt of perfumes, scented by oils and flowers. A rare waft of femininity for his nose to experience as their long straight hair dangled before his face.

"It has not been an easy year, if not several, for your house, has it?" the one on the right confirmed. "Your father's reign has been an unfruitful one, has it not? War, famine, death, and poverty."

"In no small part to the deeds of your father," the bedridden prince suggested.

"Our fathers have warred with each other, it's true, but that does not mean we should be enemies," the one on the left said, placing her hand on his. "We are no more responsible for our father's actions than you are for yours, would you not agree?"

"I suppose," he said, suspicious of their visit. But again, he reminded himself, this was all pushing beyond the realms of politeness and formality if they were merely here to kill him.

"We are neighbours, you and we," the one on the right said, placing her hand on his other hand. "We should be close, don't you think?"

"I suppose," he found himself saying again.

"We were most sorry to hear of your older brother," the one on the left said, "falling as he bravely led an assault on the wildfolk that had been raiding the rural outskirts of your city's surrounding lands. Such a brave prince would have made a good king. King Essebert the fourth, he would have been. If only your father, King Essebert the third, had cultivated the kind of relationship with his neighbouring king, where he would have felt comfortable asking for aid on such an endeavour, your big brother might still be alive, instead of falling to such savages who'd grown so bold and numerous under his ineffectual rule."

"If only your heretical father hadn't gone to war with the Order of Light, my father might have felt safe doing so," Andred replied.

"It was the knights of Paliador who went from lord to lord of our kingdom and incited rebellion," the half-elf on the right said. "Only the Order of Light would have the gall to call a response to treason, heresy. A heretic who stood trial for defending his home."

"A heretic who unnaturally survived burning at the stake. A rare feat indeed amongst those who dabble in no darkness, and even then-"

"Our father is quite a resilient man," the princess to his left said, dismissing the impossible event rather flippantly. "I suppose that's what they get for choosing such a cruel method of murder. Perhaps the gods, the order claims to represent, disagreed with that attempt to usurp power from the rightful king of Southmarch and spared him from the flames of the tortuous pyre built to slowly scorch him to death."

"Then what?" Andred asked, grimacing cynically. "Was it the gods who raised an army of the dead in an act of divine poetic irony to avenge you father for the accusations of necromancy laid at his feet?"

The pair of matching princesses looked to each other and shrugged. "Perhaps," they said in unison.

"Dead soldiers that invaded the kingdom of Cliffguard and thinned our numbers."

"Numbers wasted on a war at the order's behest. It is the Order of Light who did to this kingdom all that has befallen it. Not our father. All he ever did was defend his throne," the Aeligis sister on the left said. "Your father was the one who attacked him as he recovered from a failed rebellion. Your father was the one who sent men to ambush our brother, Prince Garykk, during a hunting trip on his birthday."

"What?" Andred asked, shocked by the accusation. "I heard he'd been taken, but… my *father*?"

"Hand on our hearts, truth," the one on the right said, as each took one of his hands and placed it over their leather-clad chests. "For it was we who rescued him. We slew all but two of the mercenaries who took him."

"Then," the other said, "of the two we captured, we slowly tortured one in front of the other. For days, without questions, only the preview of whatever hell they agreed to later attend when they came for our blood. Men who make such powerful enemies often fail to comprehend the many layers of undiscovered pain their bodies are capable of expressing. We enjoyed taking that coinblade fool on that long, long journey of discovery. He even composed a song for it, singing as he did for days on end. We accompanied him, playing his nerves like the strings of a lute. Unfortunately, we failed to learn the words of that song, having gagged his mouth. But when we grew bored, and our performance came to an end, we let them sing a new song. A song with words that spoke of your father's coin in their hands. That and a ransom to be sent to our father to deliver a fortune to another party. We then of course captured him as well."

"The tortured man was in no fit state to travel," the other sister said, "but his kidnapping cohort and the ransom collector were introduced. Not for the first time as it transpired. Then they were brought here to this very palace. Reunited with your father, the king of Cliffguard, who made no denials. Furthermore, he will confess his crimes in the morning in Hillspear Square before his people. Then he shall be executed."

"An honest end to a king who blames others for his own ill choices," her sister added.

"And, assuming you have indeed brought these events into motion, you have either come here to gloat or make some deal, is that it?" the bed-ridden prince asked.

"A deal seems like such an underestimation of what we plan to offer you," the one on the left said. "For it seems to us that you have been neglected in this bed, in this forgotten room. Guards do not stand directly outside that door, merely within the corridor. Elsewise, we'd need whisper far softer. But when your brother died…"

"Our condolences again," the one on the right interjected.

"You father," the other continued, "seemingly made no attempt to elevate or prioritise you. For you lay here, alone, unwed, and malnourished. If either of us were laid out in a bed with naught else to do, but eat and sleep, I should like to believe we would be fatter than a force-fed swine prepared for some festival feast."

"My father…" Andred began, meaning to steer the conversation elsewhere, could not deny their words. He had to admit the women before him had struck a nerve. "It is true. While I had a brother to be groomed for king, who could hunt, dance, and attend events easily, there was little reason to remember me. Then, when that brother fell, my father was too busy grieving."

"And scheming," one of the sisters added. "Scheming and committing reckless acts that would likely plunge out two kingdoms into a war yours would not survive."

"But like our brother, you are turned forty," the other said. "How is it that you've been left here without a wife to look after you and care for you."

"We have servants for that," he said, barely committed to the defence against their premise.

"But they do not care for you in a manner a wife would."

"I was struck ill at an early age, and while some were sent from the order with knowledge of healing to cure me, they merely stopped the disease, not the damage it caused. I imagine there are few outside these halls who would even remember that I exist at all. Too few within, it seems as well, I must admit. There are no princesses nor ladies of other houses who have asked after me, nor lord and kings who offered such union. For all that I have heard, and for what little that I've seen, I find it surprising that no ambition to marry into such a lucrative line has outweighed condemning oneself or daughter to life with one condemned to this bed. I suspect they doubt my ability to produce heirs."

"Your brother produced heirs, did he not?" the left sister asked.

"Two, I believe," the right sister answered.

"One fell with my brother in the attack on the wildfolk raiders, compounding my father's grief," Andred said.

"But not yours?" the left sister asked.

"Of course, it did, though I barely knew the lad," he admitted. "Neither of my nephews nor niece have ever visited me up here in this forgotten room. They saw me at feasts and weddings, when someone had the wherewithal to remember to wheel me into attendance. There and then, I was lucky to receive the odd nod from most who should have been far closer. But no one really wanted to remember that I existed, nor be made sad by that reminding during otherwise joyous occasions. I love them, for sharing the same blood, but have no relationship with them."

"And your remaining nephew and niece are too young to rule after you father, are they not?" the left sister confirmed.

"So, the throne passes to you instead, yes?" the right sister asked.

"A rule of succession in this kingdom, I'm sure most would be happy to forget as easily as they have forgotten *me* altogether."

"Then we'll make sure your father reminds them and names you heir before he takes his final breath," the left sister said, running a finger down Andred's side from his chest down slowly to his knee. "But first we must know, from just how far down you still have feeling."

"All the way," the prince said. "I have lost the use of my legs and nothing else. I still feel my toes when they are cold, or when one of the servant's trims my toenails distracted enough to take a little skin with it. Somehow, all but myself, seem to be under the impression that I'm some brainless corpse, waiting to die. I may not be able to stand and fight, but I'm still a man."

"Good," the sisters said in slow unison.

Andred looked to the smiling women sat upon his bed, still holding his hands, now stroking his legs, gently. "So, after all this time, am I to believe the two most beautiful women I have ever seen mean to offer up some lady loyal to their kin, to take my hand as queen?"

"No," the one on the right said, shaking her head.

"We mean to offer you *us*?" the other said.

"One of *you*?" he confirmed, raising his eyebrows in disbelief.

"No," the one on the left said again.

"We mean to offer you *us*?" the other said.

Andred swallowed, half believing this now to be a dream of some sort. "Both of you?"

"One a queen, the other a mistress," the left one said, with a seductive smile.

"The choice is yours, which shall serve as which," the right one clarified, raising an eyebrow with a suggestive grin.

"Our blood will make your children strong, and live longer than anyone else in your house," the left sister claimed. "One of us will make you powerful princes, and the other; powerful bastards, who'll protect them from the inevitable ambitions of other parties that will likely be whispered into the ears of your niece and nephew."

"And what will be whispered into *my* children's ears?" Andred asked.

"Your line will be bent to our will," the right sister confessed. "Make no mistake about it. But the pleasure you experience will be unlike any you could have ever hoped to know. For while we know how to make a man suffer beyond his darkest nightmares, also we can bring the brightest delights to challenge your most indulgent desires."

Andred felt his heart pounding in his chest as their words made the hairs on the back of his neck stand. He again forced a swallow to alleviate his drying throat. "Oh… I see."

"We want stability between our kingdoms, and this union would aid with that," the left sister said, leaning closer to him.

She placed his hand on her thigh, as the other sister did the same. "We will make you so many offspring, your heir will have a small army of quarter-elven half-siblings to stand by their side. At least two children for every year moving forwards, you'll be soon surrounded by all the love that has been neglected of you. Along with us of course."

"We shall be ever present to protect you," the right sister promised, "with our own loyal men and women to guard you."

"The two of you could have anyone and be anything," Andred said. "You would both choose this life? To be bound so to a cripple?"

"Our blood is half Ijcari," the left sister reminded him. "We shall live to see centuries. By the time your own heir lives to take the throne in your shadow, we shall still be young and fertile with many options before us. Women who've birthed princes and knights are not so damaged goods to loose all value. We have several lives to live if we so choose, but we shall be with you until the end, and train your children to fight and guide them until we are no longer needed here."

"Or perhaps we'll grow to like this place and stay until the end of our own days, well beyond your own," the right sister said, stroking the side of his face. "But yours will be a life of pure pleasure. We'll bring you wine and food fitting for a king. We'll bring you down to every event and occasion to feast and laugh in merriment. You will have to make the odd decree, and give the occasional order, preside over ceremony, and name knights and lords, but between those acts of duty that we cannot perform on your behalf or eventually your children's, you will be up here. Not trapped in solitude in a room you no doubt equate to a prison, but a place of unrelenting pleasure and bliss. There will be no waking moment, for as long as you endure, in which you will not know joy."

Prince Andred looked to both of them, their faces dangerously close to his own. They gently swayed their heads as their hands ran over his shoulders and chest, while he massaged the soft leather over their inner thighs. "I suppose, the only question is who to choose as wife, and who to choose as mistress."

"In this room, it will make no difference to you," the one on the left said. "One of us will adopt the surname Belethon and carry the title of queen. She shall sit beside you at official engagements, while the other will be close by, if not training the small army you'll put inside us."

"Still… an important decision," the prince said, intoxicated by their promises. "Surely, between you, you have some idea who might be more appropriate for the task?"

The pair stood up again, on either side of his bed and began to unbuckle their armour. "Again, it won't really make a difference in this room," the one on the left said, as she gently rested her belt and swords on the floor, "but neither has more nor less qualities to make a better queen."

"So, perhaps make the decision on some less tangible whim," the other said, placing her leather chest piece on a chair. "If the burden of decision is to fall to you, let the burden of who can please you more, fall to us," she said, sliding her tunic over her head to reveal two small perfect breasts.

"Perhaps you like the look of one of us more," the one left said, stepping out of her leggings, to reveal her smooth pale legs.

"Or the touch," the right princess said, bending her elegant figure over to lower her weapons as she jostled her hips out of her armour.

"Or the smell," the left sister said, now completely stood naked before him as she pulled back his sheets. Her long smooth body brushing against his legs as she climbed over them and began to slide his nightshirt up.

"Or the taste," the right sister offered as she climbed into the bed beside him, guiding his hand between her legs.

"Or we can just draw straws," the left sister said, moving her own hand up his leg.

"Do I smell flowers?" a chamber maid asked, waking Andred in the morning as she began to pull his sheets. "If I didn't know…" she paused, shocked by the sight of his residual arousal. "Pleasant dreams, my prince?"

"Ah, very," he said, embarrassed at first, then proud as the memory of the previous night quickly resurfaced. The greatest night of his life without even remote competition. "I have a good feeling about today."

"Clearly," she said, awkwardly trying to look anywhere else as she performed her daily morning tasks.

He heard the voice of Sir Barret echoing down the corridor as he ordered others. A knight of his father's royalguard who seemed to always be the one to come and tell him when something important was happening, on the rare occasions he was deemed worthy of being informed.

"Good morning, my prince," he said, impatiently gesturing more maids in. "There's to be some important announcement in the square, and *all* members of the royal family are required in attendance," he said, holding up a note. "By your father's decree."

"Even me?" Andred asked, innocently. Barely an act as he only half believed what been promised of events yet to come.

"He names you specifically," Sir Barret said, insultingly surprised.

"Well, we better not keep him waiting then."

In the main square of the city of Hillspear, men of the cityguard used their armoured bodies to fence off the curious public who gathered in the streets at the sound of bells. Nobility and royalty congregated within a partitioned section of the square, surrounded by their loyal housegaurd. Prince Andred was carried in a chair built on long handles. Until now, he'd always felt like some piece of furniture being brought into the rare event he was allowed to attend. But today, he felt like some ancient emperor. Even if no one else thought of him as more than some invalid or burden to be forgotten or ignored.

Andred looked to his nephew and niece, young enough to be excited to be there without question. He looked to their mother, his sister by law, still wearing black. She had lost her husband and firstborn in one fell swoop. He pitied her, though the woman had barely spoken more than a handful of words to him during the entirety of her courtship and marriage to his late brother, whose visits quickly diminish from frequent to never under her influence.

Prince Andred looked back to other parties and saw Southmarch soldiers, large and foreboding, descended from invaders from the cold continent of Craguhr, beyond the south sea, who had helped seat House Aeligis as the ruling line of conquered neighbouring kingdom. They surrounded the twin half-frost elf princesses who had visited upon the prince in the night. He wanted nothing more than to look upon them to bring the memory of last night into sharp focus but refused to let his eyes wander in their direction. The waft of conspiracy was already in the air. A scent he hoped no other would notice and wished not to make it seem as though it came from him.

Two men stood on a platform. Shackled and in little more than rags, their faces and bodies bore many injuries for all to see. Bruises and grazes showed while deeper wounds were bandaged. Their eyes darkened by insufficient sleep and their faces browbeaten, their spirits broken. They seemed two standing corpses waiting to be released from the torment of their existence.

Lord Brantyn Ebralund, Master of Justice, emerged from an overlooking balcony attached to a tower from which announcements into the square were typically made. He cleared his throat as he unfurled a rolled parchment. "People of Hillspear, nobility of the kingdom of Cliffguard, I bring forward two condemned men. Their crime is one against the neighbouring kingdom of Southmarch, but its implications have endangered peace with that kingdom, thereby making their crime one against our own. They did kidnap Garykk Aeligis, prince of Southmarch, and heir to its throne. Committing a conspiracy against an allied sovereignty is tantamount to treason, and so no punishment can be more lenient than death itself. The manner of that death and mercy of its delivery will be determined by their confession and naming of co-conspirators."

The crowd mumbled and chattered. They had had an inconsistent relationship with the kingdom to the east, over the years, and the Aeligis name had long carried a shadow. Another war with them was to be feared, for the dark things they had all been told, yet love for that kingdom was also rare. The crowd of peasants could give no clear response of emotion, but their intrigue was obvious. Not the normal certainty of crowd participation the city was used to hosting on such occasions.

"Secure the ease of your passing with a swift death by naming the one who hired you, mercenaries," the Master of Justice called down to them. "By whose coin were you sent to make so criminally grand an undertaking?"

One of the clearly tortured men raised his head, looking to the balcony. "King Essebert Belethon the third," he announced.

Loud gasps and increased chatter issued from the gathered crowd. Anger stirred as the assembly refused to believe such an accusation, clearly assuming the men to be in further contempt of their hosts. With the recent death of their beloved Prince Essebert the fourth and his son, the fifth, they were quick to call for a prolonged and tortuous end.

Prince Andred's gathered relatives equally scoffed, uttering comments of immediate dismissal and insult to their shared name. While none consulted him nor made conversation in his direction, Andred made no remark and shared no expression. He merely surveyed the crowd, and all gathered, curious to see how things were going to play out. He was sceptical that any of what the twin princesses did say could possibly come to pass. In part, he believed it some sick joke.

Lord Ebralund's mouth was agape in shock as he stared down for some time at the arrested pair. "Do you mean to further incriminate yourselves with such treasonous slander?" he angrily demanded. "How dare you make such…" the Master of Justice turned as another stepped out onto the balcony.

Prince Andred's own father, the king, stood upon the balcony, looking down onto the city's townsfolk, guards, and his kin alike. He seemed troubled and in deep thought. He looked down briefly to the twins, also quick to break from a prolonged gaze, and looked to his palace instead. The crowd cheered for him, though it was polluted by the insults many of them were still slinging at the pair of accused men. The king held his hand out to invite a silence that obediently soon settled over the peasants. Andred's young nephew pointed excitedly to the king, saying "Look, it's grandfather," to his sister.

"My father fought against the kingdom of Southmarch many years ago," the king said to his people. "That war thinned our numbers and left cities populated as if towns, towns as if villages, and villages as if camps. When I inherited the throne from the man who raised me, I brought with him much of the bitterness he cultivated against our neighbours. In the two decades I have ruled, I have seen our beloved kingdom struggle as it never truly recovered from the war and, being my father's son, I have laid much blame on the kingdom of Southmarch and its king. When my eldest son, your future king, fell fighting the wildfolk, and my grandson along with him… it was too much. From that moment, knowing my legacy was lost, broke me as a man." He wrapped his fingers tightly around the balcony's railing as he sighed to himself. "In my grief, I lashed out at the one upon whom I had always favoured laying blame for all ills that fell upon the kingdom, for a stronger force would have quelled the wildfolk rebellion with far fewer losses. And so, yes, I, your king, King Essebert the third, made a wild decision to have Prince Garykk Aeligis of Southmarch kidnapped and ransomed as an act of petty spite, unbefitting a regent of so fine a land."

The crowd were devastated by the revelation. The king's family and surrounding lords were also stunned. Some more than others, it seemed. Andred's nephew and niece looked to their mother in confusion, seeking some explanation, too young to truly understand the events unfolding before them.

"To make this right, I shall submit to punishment for this crime, having imperilled the kingdom I am charged with protecting. I do this to stave off retaliation that would harm my people and what remains of my family. My judgment has been reckless and without counsel, and I hope you think kindly upon me for attempting to rectify these misdeeds. I name my second son, my successor and heir." He looked and pointed to his son upon a chair from which he could not stand. "Prince Andred Belethon, the fourth to carry that name. I name you the next king of Cliffguard. May your rule be free of the bitterness that tainted your father's and grandfather's."

Still shocked that what he was told had come to pass so far, even Andred was uncertain how much of his own surprised face was genuine and how much was rehearsed, as he felt all eyes fall upon him. None in the royal party present said a word. There was a deafening silence. A man to whom none had made any attempt to cultivate a relationship would be ruler now. He felt his brother's widow look to her children, placing her hands on their shoulders before she looked to him. But he did not look back. He simply stared at his father. Not wishing to see the many other faces about. For he envisioned no facial expression that would flatter him. Not from any party. He would not sully the announcement with faces that told of misgiving, incomprehension, and jealously. He imagined no reverence awaiting him and would give no one the satisfaction of receiving their dropped jaws and scandalised brows.

"I hope that your rule will steer the kingdom from the path of ruin my father set us on," the king continued, hushing the mumbling of the crowds. "Make peace once and for all with Southmarch, however you may. Foster a bond between the two southernmost kingdoms of the Umberlands."

He was all but telling him to marry one of the twin princesses, Andred realised. It seemed he too had been visited upon by them, but in some far less pleasurable meeting in which he was somehow convinced and coaxed into making this sacrifice. Did they make threats or simply lay out the reality of what would follow if there was another instalment of war between their kingdoms. Still looking to the balcony that held his father, he nodded. "I shall do all that I can to repair our boundaries and ties," he promised, yelling back. His voice carried, bouncing off stone and filling the square. A voice unknown to the people, and barely known to his family. A new voice to the kingdom, that had laid unheard and forgotten in a near deserted wing of the palace for decades.

"I know you will, son," the king said. There was a genuine tenderness in the king's voice Andred had not heard from his father in a long time. The king looked to the two mercenaries who stood looking exhausted. "In hiring these men, I have wrought upon them their deaths. Though they are men who serve only coin, they are men of my kingdom, and I shall share their fate, and make no delay about it. Farewell."

The king stepped away and disappeared inside the tower, leaving all to contribute to the great noise of speculative and uncertain chatter amongst the great gathering. Even the guards looked to each other, wondering what any of what had unfolded truly meant.

Andred, still loath to look to the women with whom he'd made a pact, found little where else to cast his eyes. He still felt eyes upon him within his own party but instead looked to the crowds and guards amongst whom chaos reigned in layers of unintelligible conversation. He saw faces in the crowd look to him, curious. Several of the guards met his gaze and nodded when they saw him look upon them. Then lowering their eyes in reverent obedience. Andred still expected no such respect from any within the royal party, again only laying eyes upon the members of houseguard who lowered their heads to him.

By the time the king appeared on the platform where the two mercenaries stood, an executioner waited. His head draped in a black hood and carrying a long handled heavy axe. The two men submitted to the block and their heads were taken in a basket. Few cheers issued, as the strange circumstance unfolded, but noise was still made. Uncertain and confused, the crowd watched on as the executioner wiped clean his hafted blade of peasant blood.

Then the king stood before the great wooden block and shook his head as he looked down upon the basket that was taken away and replaced with a fresh one. While he shared their fate, his head would not share a receptacle. He took a few deep breaths and stood there a while, where no guard nor the executioner made to rush him as they typically would one condemned. The square was silent in disbelief. All eyes were upon the king, taking his final breaths as he composed himself. He looked distant, staring off into nowhere as he seemingly pondered. Finally, he gave a nod and stepped to the block. "May the Twelve forgive me and protect in my stead my family, my city, my people, and my kingdom," he called out with a sad smile.

When he crouched down by the block and placed his head upon it ready, all the city guard lowered their heads. Andred's sister-by-law pulled her children in and covered their eyes and she looked to the future king who watched, somewhat in disbelief himself. No further words of guidance came from the king for his newly named successor. He patiently waited, holding the sides of the block with his unbound hands. It was a stark and strange sight; a king who condemned himself to death.

Though the executioner hesitated, the king's head left his body, as did an extraordinary amount of blood from his neck. A quick and gruesome end to the man who had raised Andred. At least to a point, before slowly forgetting he even existed.

A dark red sheet of some thick material was cast over the king's body, quickly covering him. The crowd stood stunned. Their faces filled with uncertainty. All that had happened was barely believable to Andred as the sensation of knowing he had move so suddenly from a forgotten invalid's bed to the highest chair in the kingdom. A coronation would take place soon, but it seemed traditional at the time of a king's death for someone to shout 'the king is dead, long live the king' but in the stunned silence those words issued from no mouth.

Nevertheless. He was now king.

Barend Nieuwstraten III writes primarily within the realms of fantasy, science fiction, and horror. Published in over thirty anthologies, he continues to work on short stories, stand-alone novels, and an epic series. Born to Dutch and Indian immigrants he resides in Sydney, Australia.

Impressions

by August Blaine Centauri

box of tissues flies at my head, and I duck, just grateful it's not anything more destructive. "You can stop doing that," Mira Midnight snaps at me, using her real voice instead of her put-on TV voice.

I glare at her as the tissue box falls harmlessly to the ground. "I'm not doing anything. You're the fraud that likes to put on shows."

"I do not put on shows!" Mira snaps, so distracted with glaring back at me that she misses the charging cable and it hits her dead on the back of the head. I probably could have helped my snort of laughter, but I didn't see a reason to pretend I didn't find it funny. It's a charging cable. No damage done. It flops uselessly to the ground. "Hey!" Mira's glare intensifies.

All I can do is roll my eyes. "This is what happens when you get involved in things you know nothing about." I shrug and bat away the kitchen towels threatening me.

"Nothing? Nothing? This is MY job," she screeches at me. "I get paid for this sort of thing. You're the one out of your depth."

"Then why are you the one panicking over nothing?" I grumble, only partially under my breath.

"I am *not* panicking," Mira says unconvincingly, a note of hysteria in her voice as she kicks at the couch pillow flopping around her feet.

Taking a slow, deep breath in, I close my eyes and resist the urge to taunt the utterly taunt-able TV (aka "fake") psychic and medium Mira Midnight. If we keep this up, all we'll achieve is feeding the impression currently attempting to torment us. The more we feed the impression, the more power it will get, and then we will have a real problem. This impression isn't strong enough to do actual damage to us, but it will become stronger if we provide it with enough frustration, anger, and other emotions. A fleece blanket taps my legs as I let out a slow breath. It's not just taunting when I say that Mira is unequipped to deal with this situation, no matter how much money she's scamming out of our poor client. Mira is a fraud. She's not psychic or a medium, and any spiritual knowledge she has is more than likely common misinformation she got from unreliable websites that exist to scam people in the same way Mira does.

Deciding to just ignore Mira instead of engage with her, I open my eyes once I feel a bit more calm. There are lots of ways to cleanse negative energy, which is basically what many impressions are. I use salt water a lot because it's easy to come by and carry around. It's also more subtle than whipping out a bundle of herbs to burn. Focusing on my energy flow and meditating to get some good energy flowing about the house, I find my small spray bottle and start spritzing salt water about.

It doesn't take long for the air to start feeling lighter and cleaner. Impressions are what the uninformed would call ghosts. In my experience, and I've been sensitive ever since I can remember, ghosts as media portrays them simply don't exist. I don't fully know what happens when people die, but their spirit doesn't stick around in any meaningful way. When someone has a lot of emotions around their death, as is common in sudden and/or violent deaths, their spirit does leave behind an impression of their moment of death or something important they were thinking about before they died.

An impression is kind of akin to a recording. Impressions are a representation of those feelings or memories, existing as a manifested repetitive loop until it finally loses energy and dissipates. Mostly, impressions disappear pretty quickly - typically within a year. It's the rare instance where an impression can last for decades or even centuries. Usually, when that happens, it's because living people are interacting with the impression, fueling it with their emotions and helping to power the remanent as an energy battery.

It may come as a surprise to others but being sensitive didn't afford me much popularity as a kid. In particular, I have a good eye for impressions and energy. I also have premonitory dreams now and then, but my life is usually mundane enough that it's not even worth mentioning. It was being able to see and interact with impressions othered me from my peers. The more othered I felt, the more I turned to these impressions for comfort and company. As one might imagine, that became a cycle that took me many years to break out of. Inspired by TV, I often tried to communicate with these impressions. I wanted to help them fulfill their purpose so they could move on.

Thing is, impressions never interacted back with me. There were no tears or long life stories or last tasks they admitted to needing to perform. Nobody shared any words to pass onto their loved ones. They might freeze and appear to stare at me, but I later figured out that this was just the impression orienting towards the nearest source of energy (me). It did take me an embarrassingly long time to accept that there was nothing I could do to communicate with impressions because they weren't sentient or aware.

They were just fading snapshots of a previously living soul. Now, if you feed them lots of energy, they will grow more out of control and appear to act in a more thoughtful and autonomous way. Suppressed memories start floating to the surface and impacting their behavior. All of the behavior is either left-behind patterns from the living body or reacting to stimuli in the environment, like throwing objects at Mira and I because our emotions are creating a lot of energy.

"What, is that holy water or something? Dressed like that," she references the goth aesthetic I've leaned into since high school as a defense mechanism against the judgement I was receiving anyway, "I certainly didn't take you for the religious type." Mira's voice cuts through my thoughts as the impression shrinks with the shrinking energy availability.

Resisting the urge to roll my eyes, I continue doing my best to ignore her. Our client may have forced us to both be here at the same time, but I cannot be forced to actually work with Mira, who only makes a mockery of my life. "You know, I don't think we're being recorded. You don't have to put on so much of a show. We could just hang here for a bit and tell Priscilla everything's all exorcised in a bit." I ground my teeth but still refuse to engage. There's no purpose in calling this ridiculous woman out.

I've hated Mira Midnight since the first time I saw her crop up on TV when we were both seventeen and heard that fake, raspy, slow-tempo voice spewing out lies and manipulation. Mother laughed and said I was just jealous she was making a real living off of what kids at school hated me for when I made the mistake of admitting my feelings to her one day. Being twice that age now, I can admit that mother wasn't totally wrong. It does infuriate me that people are willing to worship at Mira's feet when she's just a snake oil salesman.

Those feelings weren't helped by the fact that I'd been experiencing taunting, mocking, and bullying for actually being able to do what Mira claimed she could do, including by my own mother. In my 30s, I can now also admit that Mira's mom clearly groomed her to rip people off so she could collect her own generous paycheck off of Mira's work. If Mira as an adult didn't continue to choose to rob grieving people, I might even work up some pity for her.

"You want me to turn on all the sinks in this house and flood it? That'd be extra effective."

She's obviously trying to rile me up. It's frustratingly effective. "Nobody is making you stay. Please, feel free to leave."

"So you can tell Priscilla and get the whole check for yourself?" Mira actually has the audacity to laugh. "No, thanks." See? Shouldn't have engaged at all.

I like using a quartz and obsidian mix for keeping spaces cleansed. Finishing with the water bottle, I pick out a few strategic spots and stick a tumbled piece of quartz or obsidian around the home by windows for sun charging. With the sun charging them daily, they'll continue to cleanse for a while and should help this impression either migrate to another location or completely dissipate.

Our client, Miss Priscilla, tracked down both Mira and I in regards to a haunting she believed she was experiencing. This should do the trick for her. I normally don't do this sort of work for others - I generally don't find it necessary since most haunting experiences and the like are greatly exaggerated, and impressions dissipate fairly quickly on their own - but Miss Priscilla was insistent and she'd seemed terribly scared. Guilt stayed my hand from saying no.

"Okay. Now we can go," I inform Mira, feeling only trace amounts of the impression present.

"Oh, goody! Thanks, boss," Mira insufferably responds. She pokes at one of the crystals I put down, and my fingers twitch with the automatic urge to smack her hand away, but she picks her bag up and starts to lead us out of the house.

That's when I realize Miss Priscilla probably never really cared about the impression in her house. Mira screams at the large man in a ski mask who steps through the door and blocks our exit. Rapidly backpedalling, she quickly steps on my foot and runs straight into me. Backing up is undoubtedly a better plan than my brain's plan of freezing. I can't tear my eyes away from the large pin prominently displayed on the intruder's shirt. We've been set-up. I recognize that pin. Mira is yanking at my arm, trying to get me to follow her. The pin signifies a supposed secret society type group. The kind of secret society type group that you never want to have a run-in with.

Mira lets me go as the man steps closer. Then the asshole holds up a taser and tases me. Lightning fire pain lances through my body like pissed off bees bouncing around under my skin as I lose control and fall to the ground, shaking and shivering. It feels like forever that I'm tased. Although I have no intention or ability to move when the shock finally stops, the asshole steps forward and calmly kicks me in my head. I don't even have time to feel the pain for that.

When I finally become aware, the pain makes itself known with a ferocity, ripping me into a consciousness full of suffering. My head is pounding so badly, my heart feels like it's in my head. I moan and try to get into a position to vomit. That's when I realize that I'm bound and gagged and going nowhere. My throat feels thick and scratchy. I swallow thickly around the gag, trying to avoid having to asphyxiate on my own vomit.

A matching moan sounds from behind me and fingertips gently feel out my hands and pat them in what I guess is meant to be comforting. Mostly, I find it surprising, weakly jerking against the bonds. It takes a moment for thoughts to clarify through the pain in my head. Realizing I must be tied to Mira, I slouch back down. Breathing in through my nose, I try to calm myself and take actual stock of my situation. We're in a dimly lit basement. A symbol, seemingly painted in blood, is centered under where Mira and I sit. Though I can't tell what it is from this position, I have my suspicions. The rotten smell of death permeates the air - and it's not helping the nausea. It's so cliche it hurts.

I hypothesize the symbol under us is a pentagram painted right over a spiral. The secret society. Their symbol is messy and busy. It's a pentagram on top of a spiral, sort of making an 'eight' together. To the left is a stylized chicken head. To the right is a stylized headless chicken body. They call themselves The Lowlings, a self-deprecating knock both on what they view as their unfortunate place in the world and to where they turned to gain power. Their society is a bastardization of satanism, TV hoodoo, TV voodoo, and probably a few other religions and spiritual practices I'm not familiar with. In essence, it's white people bullshit cooked up by angry, entitled white people who feel wronged by others and abandoned by the christian God. Instead of doing anything to create actual change in the world, they get together and make each other even angrier and try to invoke other powers to grant them the privilege they believe they deserve and don't already wield.

They're awful, of course, but I've always written them off as a pathetic joke. Angry white people are everywhere and plenty dangerous. Everyone gave them wide berth in the magic and crystal shops, but for the most part, they just seemed like a lot of bluster and bluff. Obviously, that's what they wanted everyone to think. I had no idea Miss Priscilla was associated with them at all. She has to be; I cannot picture her being tricked into trapping me and Mira if she wasn't actually a part of the group. As if on cue, noisy footsteps stomp down the stairs. "Welcome, dearies," Miss Priscilla smiles wide as she reaches the bottom. Her smile more mirrors the wolf that eats the grandma than it does a friendly grandma.

Six others are with Miss Priscilla. No ski masks in sight. The hulking man who subdued Mira and me is obvious. He stands at least a foot taller than everyone else and is twice as wide. Middle-aged, he's got black, slicked back hair. He feels like a man who thought he'd make it big in the NFL, never made it, and became a used car salesman instead. The other five are comprised mostly of men, with only one other woman besides Miss Priscilla. The sneer on her young face makes it seem like she's smelling sewage. Perhaps she's not sneering and the carcass stench is upturning her nose.

The four other men range from what looks like my age to Miss Priscilla's sixty or seventy. None of them bring up any memories or spark of recognition for me. "Oh, how rude of us. Of course you can't talk with those gags in your mouth. Ah well," she says cheerily. How much she is enjoying this situation sends an involuntary shudder up my spine. "We don't really need you to speak, anyway. We just need people with your particular skill sets." My mind is still moving slowly, so it takes me a moment to understand her. When I do, I give an unladylike snort. It's almost funny. Mira and I are about to be sacrificed - murdered - because we're both supposedly sensitive. Even if I thought their ridiculous ritual had any basis, it wouldn't even work. Mira's not even a little sensitive.

Miss Priscilla's eyes narrow at my snort. "John: begin," she says, nodding towards me. Mira squeals and begins squirming. Her rocking movements only jar the pit in my stomach. I moan piteously and squeeze my eyes shut. She may not be sensitive, but I can't claim she doesn't have any skills. Presumably understanding she was only hurting me, Mira stills. The whimpering doesn't stop. Her hands twist and yank at the ropes, which makes them chafe against my skin. I look dully up at John as he stands over me. His hair is salt and pepper. I see no humanity or compassion in his eyes. He's the type of man my mother would find handsome, which does no more to endear him to me than whatever he's about to do.

Perhaps it's because of pain or because of what I endured as a child or Mira's panic, but I stay calm even when John pulls the hunting knife out and kneels down in front of me. I lock my eyes onto his, but he's focused on his task. One hand reaches out and holds my arm still. He deftly draws the knife over my skin. The fairly shallow, inch long cut, horizontal above my bicep, makes me breathe out forcefully through my nose, but it's otherwise not bad. It's nothing compared to the pain in my head, and it's heaps better than slitting my throat, which is what I was expecting. John rubs the knife against my skin, smearing the knife with more blood. Face deadly serious, John stands, backs out of the symbol painted on the ground, then flicks the knife over the symbol. Drops of my blood splatter across the ground and my legs.

Mira does not stay quite so calm or quiet when it's her turn, but tied to me, there's not much she can do to resist. The Lowlings gather in a circle around the symbol painted on the ground. They all reach out their hands, palms facing in towards the center of the circle, and begin chanting in a language that I'm not positive is real but is obviously rehearsed as well as their tempo syncs. There is no doubt in my mind that this ritual is meant to be long and slow. They certainly intend to kill Mira and I by the end of it, but there will be plenty of time for torture.

Behind me, Mira is still squirming. I wish she would stop so that I might think more clearly. With my head the way it is, I can rule out any physical fighting. Even if I could fight, two against seven aren't great odds, especially when one of those seven is twice the size of both Mira and I. Running doesn't seem like it's going to be great for me either, but it'll be the best bet if we can just get free. It's the getting free part seems insurmountable.

There's really no way for Mira and I to secretly steal a knife, which would be about the only thing I can think of to get us out of the mass of thick rope looping around us, up and down our arms. However, I'm not totally defenseless. I cleansed the upstairs, but that's not a complete guarantee that a house won't be host to the energy of death. There's a lot of strong emotion in this basement right now. Mira's fear, my anger, the excitement and even the impotent rage of The Lowlings. I stoke the anger in my chest, breathing into it and letting it eke out into the environment when I breathe out.

Being sensitive - being a medium - in real life isn't nearly as dramatic as it can be in movies. There's no actual crackle or spark of energy. No portal - to hell or otherwise - opens up. A demon doesn't appear and offer me a contract to save my life. From the outside, it looks like all I'm doing is mindful breathing. On the inside, I am manipulating energy, helping it grow more intense and reach out towards the edges of the basement. I use the energy to call out to any and all impressions.

Since impressions don't have any intelligence, I can't control them. I can't ask them to do anything specific. I can only draw them to the basement, like an anglerfish luring in prey, let them wreck havoc, and hope it works out in my favor. Of course, this hinges on there being nearby impressions to lure into my trap. Much like fishing, it is a task of patience.

I have not managed to snag any impressions by the time the chanting changes. This time it's a blond, preppy man who approaches me with a knife. I growl in my throat, letting my anger and fear bleed through. Now is not the time to be stoic. This time, I scream, and I'm not acting it up. The blade of this man's knife sinks deep across my chest. He draws the knife from collarbone to collarbone and coarsely rubs his stubby fingers around the wound, uncaring of how he tears it. Mira squirms and yanks and probably makes it ten times worse on herself when it's her turn.

That's when the washing machine turns on. The Lowlings all start at the sound, stumbling over their chant. Swapping victorious grins, they find their rhythm again. Boxes and containers around the basement start shaking. It doesn't take long before the hulking man approaches me with his own knife. Fear bubbles up in me as he teases the knife across my ear. Yanking my head away from him, he actually laughs. Then he stabs the knife into my thigh, and I throw my head back and howl. Tears stream from my eyes as he purposefully wiggles the knife back and forth as he slowly draws it out of my leg. The sadistic asshole grabs onto my face and firmly pulls it down, forcing me to watch as he sticks his finger in the wound and flicks out blood at the ground several times. I slouch when he finishes with me and shudder with the force of my sobs. Mira is attempting to scoot out of the circle, but I'm deadweight sabotaging her attempts. Guilt fills me but doesn't give me the strength to move to help her efforts.

Where there is one, many may come. I vaguely register that the original impression has multiplied to five. The washer is starting and stopping. Things spilled from containers on shelves roll along the ground and begin floating in the air. Mira's stiff posture lets me know the hulking man must be in front of her, toying with her now. Then my arms go slack. A man is screaming. The six other Lowlings falter. I fall over as Mira's body suddenly disappears from behind mine. On the ground, I find myself looking up the hulking man, kneeling and screaming and clutching his eye, from which a knife handle protrudes. By the time I realize I have enough room to untangle myself from the ropes and sit up to untie my legs, Mira has tackled Miss Priscilla and stolen her knife.

With a knife to Miss Priscilla's throat, Mira's shouting for the other Lowlings to back off. The impressions are still multiplying. The washer is shaking so badly now that it's moving across the floor. Little bits and bobs and tools and flinging through the air. I stand, wobbling on one leg. "Jordan! Upstairs! Up the stairs!" Mira is shouting, and I belatedly realize she's talking to me. The wooden support beams above us groan and one of them cracks. The youngest woman becomes overwhelmed at this, and she dashes up the stairs and away from us all. One less person to worry about.

With a cold-heartedness I didn't know I possessed, I limp forward and put one hand on top of the hulking man's head and grip his hair tight. He's whimpering. His hands keep fidgeting around the knife, unsure of what to do. I take firm hold of the knife, push against his head, and slide the knife out. With a shriek, he half-heartedly lunges towards me. I hop backyards. He falls flat on his face. Grasping arms reach out for me, but I'm not worried about him.

Holding the knife out in front of me, I limp towards the basement exit. A built-in wooden shelf is ripped from the wall and slams into the ground. All The Lowlings jump. The man about Miss Priscilla's age dives for a corner and cowers there. John holds his knife out towards me, looking from me to Miss Priscilla, who can't talk for how hard Mira has the knife pressed to her throat. The hand gestures make it clear she wants the others to attack, though. I prepare to dive out of the way as John steels himself. A stray wrench clips him in the head, and he flinches and drops the knife. I rush forward and shove him. The two remaining Lowlings give up all pretenses and make their own beelines for the exit.

A wooden shelf flies through the air and barely misses me. I duck and nearly fall. A strong arm grabs me and rights me. Beside me, Mira is nothing but focus as she pulls me towards the exit, up the stairs, and towards safety. I look back and catch a glimpse of Miss Priscilla, sprawled on the floor, and a recovered John closing in on Mira and I. Then Mira gets us out of the room and kicks the door closed behind us. Reaching back, I find a lock and click it home.

Everything's a whirlwind after that. Mira helps me to Miss Priscilla's neighbor, where we call the cops and paramedics, and I don't fight it as I'm loaded up into an ambulance after a round of questioning from the cops. It surprises me when Mira stops by and asks if she can visit as I'm relaxing in a hospital bed, bandaged and stitched up, waiting for my roommate to come and pick me up. Only hesitating for a moment, I welcome her in. Seems like the least I can do after she stuck around to save me instead of just running and saving herself.

"You really weren't playing a trick with those flying objects, were you?"

I laugh before pain cuts me off. "That's what you came to talk about?"

"Well, yeah. I understand everything else that happened, but I can't work that out. I thought you had the upstairs rigged, but there's no way you had the basement rigged unless you're really that masochistic that you wanted to get stabbed just to make some point about me being a fake."

Even though I accept that I'm sensitive and frequent shops that cater to these sorts of gifts, I really don't talk about it much. Between my mother and bullies at school, I learned to bottle this subject up. Something about the raw, open curiosity in Mira's eyes releases the floodgates, and I talk - about pretty much everything. I explain impressions. I open up about how difficult others make it for you when you're actually sensitive. I even share my disdain of her job. Through it all, Mira never interrupts me or tries to defend herself. Finally, I run out of steam and, to distract her from rebutting anything I've said, I ask, "why didn't you just make a run for it? You probably could have escaped back when I was being tased."

Leaning back in her chair, Mira lets out a long, slow breath. "It didn't cross my mind, honestly. I guess I understand your feelings, but just so you know, I do this psychic thing to try and help people. Not everyone can afford a therapist or trusts them. People turn to all sorts of solutions to try to get help and closure. This is how I can help. I didn't leave because I couldn't just leave you there alone."

Now I'm angry again. "You could have called for help!"

Mira blinks rapidly. "I...guess I didn't think of that. Sorry," she says sheepishly.

My anger instantly evaporates. I snort and relax back against the bed, totally exhausted. "Yeah," I say, "I've been there before. Nobody reacts perfectly in an emergency."

After a beat, Mira speaks again. "I'm also not trying to mock you or people like you with my job," she says softly. "I've only ever thought of how I might help. I didn't realize how I might be hurting."

"It's okay," I respond automatically but find that the sentiment is actually genuine. I feel pent up years of hurt I've been carrying around with me over the years slough off my shoulders. It's not Mira's fault how my peers treated me. "I've only ever thought of my own pain. I didn't realize how you might be helping."

Leaning forward, Mira rests her hand gently on top of mine, and I freeze, afraid she might remove it if I react. The contact is soothing and reassuring. I feel a spark of surety in my soul, similar to what I feel after I dream a premonition. It feels like the start of something new.

August Blaine Centauri is a trickster in a human's body who has been spinning yarns since around three years old. Blaine has one piece published in the online literary magazine, "Spiritus Mundi Review, Issue 2: Identities". Thon is a proud weirdo. In thon spare time from working or writing, Blaine practices piano, lifts weights, and spars in Muay Thai.

Sound and Silence

by Fern KL Goodliffe

Tacey's parents wept silently, her friends and siblings gathered around and wrapped her in their arms, but Tacey stood numb. Other people from other villages trailed away, some jubilant, some, seeing Tacey and her family, trying to hide their relief.

It was Tacey who would be going to feed Grandma this year.

Guards came over. Some were the usual militia, but three stood apart, far taller and wearing wolf pelts over their armour, the wolf heads covering their own to give a terrifying visage. They escorted Tacey and her group back to Tacey's family home, and gave them the night to prepare before withdrawing, standing outside to give the mourners space while ensuring Tacey could not run.

There was silence for a while, then everyone started talking, saying how sad and shocked they were, but Tacey saw relief on more than one face; relief that it wasn't them. And contempt, though she may have imagined it. She watched a brother and one of her best friends getting steadily closer. They'd be wed and trying for a baby before long, a good way to reduce the chance of being Chosen next time. They weren't the only ones, either. The room was filled with sound and movement and the smell of too many people that merged until it became too much for Tacey, suffocating her with its intensity. She stood sharply, and walked out of the room. There was a hush, but no one followed her, and the chatter gradually resumed.

Tacey looked outside, to where the militia stood unevenly around the house, stretching and fidgeting as they needed to, and sharing words with each other. She couldn't hear the jokes, but each occasional dark chuckle was like a punch. *How dare they laugh tonight.* The wolf guards stood together, preternaturally still. If it weren't for their breath in the air, she could have mistaken them for statues. Their breath seemed to come in sync with each other, and when they turned their heads to look at her, they moved as though puppets controlled by the same string. She shuddered at the moonlight gleaming off their teeth, and ducked back inside, seeking the quiet she was named for.

No one disturbed her in the bed she'd always shared with her siblings. She hadn't expected or even intended to sleep, but she woke alone for the first time in her life, to a quiet house and the smell of baked goods. She could hear her parents and youngest sister in the kitchen, so went to join them. There was a pause, a jerk of stillness as she entered, then her father swept her to a chair and food was laid in front of her.

The eyes resting on her were all red-rimmed. She picked at the food.

The head of the militia guard and the tallest wolf man entered then. They addressed Tacey, the human guard gruff towards her and deferential to the wolf. Tacey saw the grovelling and missed the fear that powered it. She dismissed him as foolish and beneath her, and focused on the wolf. The fur-clad skull still hid most of his human face, just his lower jaw human where the wolf's had been removed. He seemed, impossibly, to be seeing through the wolf's eyes. The pelt ran down his back, the forelegs attached at his arms but the hind legs and tail bouncing free. The fur was pale, white with silvered markings, and the human skin not much darker.

The human guard handed her a crimson hooded riding cape, the uniform of the Sacrifice. "Is this food for her?" He was looking at her mother, at the basket on the table. It was filled to the brim with bread, cheese and cakes, a few apples. At her mother's nod, the guard went through the basket, checking for weapons or poisons, for anything that could help Tacey defend herself, a reminder that the Sacrifice had to be completely at Grandma's mercy. Tacey sank back into numbness as the wolf guard stepped over, took the cape from her and arranged it over her shoulders, securing it in place. His touch was surprisingly gentle, but she could discern no emotion in him.

The human guard spoke again. "Here we are then. Time to move." His tone was dismissive, almost belittling, and his face twisted as he sneered at Tacey and her family.

Tacey remained numb, feeling at the eye of the storm as everything raged around her and she remained still. It was not a peaceful stillness, but eerie and empty, even as her parents embraced her, even as the human guard wrenched her from them and the wolf guard stepped between to ensure they couldn't follow.

Tacey walked with the guards out of the house, through the small town, and out of the gates. She looked back then, and felt a shroud of fear and loneliness try to surround her. She bit the inside of her cheek hard to fend it off, and looked to the woods. Flanked by her guards, she stepped forward, focussing on the pressure of the ground under her feet, the chill in the air, the scratchy weight of the cloak. There was little bird song, but distantly a corvid shouted, and the air still held the petrichor of the previous day's rain.

The human guard grabbed her shoulder before she could walk into the shade of the trees. "So desperate to meet your fate, scrimshanker," he smirked, and went to speak further but the wolf guard interrupted him.

"Mind yourself. She is the Sacrifice. Show some respect." It was the first time Tacey had heard him speak; his voice was deep and gravelly, distorted by the mismatched jaws. The human guard shrivelled at his gaze and let his hand fall, turning to look away. The wolf guard turned to Tacey. "Well, Little One, this is where we leave you. Follow the path, and your guide will arrive. Do not deviate from the route. I am sure you have heard all the rules before, and I am sure you understand the stakes. Grandma must eat, for the sake of us all." He lowered his chin so that the golden wolf eyes met and held her brown ones, drilling the importance of his words into her. "Stick to the path." She swallowed the nervous saliva that gathered in her mouth, and nodded. He briefly bowed his head in return, then whipped around, nearly hitting her with the tail, and strode away, the human guard scurrying in his wake like a scolded squire. Tacey watched until they disappeared behind the wall, then looked to the woodland before her.

Dark trees loomed, branches ending in hand-like, clawing twigs that stretched over the path. Tacey felt a rising gulp of panic cut and let out a long, steady breath to try and control it. The red cape marked her out: no one would mess with someone on their way to Grandma's house. But she'd heard of the threats in the forest all her life, and letting go of that fear wasn't so simple. Anyway, it was easier to think about the things under the trees that weren't a threat to her than to admit to herself the fate that awaited her at the centre. She thought about all those who had stood here before her, wondered how many had turned and run. She knew some had. She couldn't blame them. But the towns they'd lived in had never been rebuilt, the ruins pockmarking the landscape as a brutal reminder of the responsibility she was now under.

She wouldn't turn and run. Not for the people who'd Chosen her – sure, choosing who to shortlist must be hard, but she'd still spit if she saw them – but for the people she cared about. Her family, her friends. The donkeys she'd see each day, carrying goods around the town. The town itself; the buildings, the streams, the trees. She looked over her shoulder. She'd never see it again, but this way it would still exist. She blew out a long, loud breath, and stepped under the canopy.

The sun seemed to fade, as weak as though behind a thick cloud though the sky remained clear. It threw the trees into jagged silhouettes, dark as shadows, sharp as the stones beside the path. The basket over one arm, she readjusted the cloak with her other. The air felt thicker yet colder. Leaves rustled in the still air, and something grunted and snuffled in the distance. It took every gram of her courage to step forward, but she thought again about all the others before her. Each footfall was easier than the last, until Tacey glanced back and saw only woodland and pathway behind her. She was sure she hadn't walked far enough, nor turned enough of a bend, to lose sight of the point where she entered, yet behind her the path led into darkening forest. Her inner world spun, and she let out a whimper as she stretched out her arms for balance. A bread roll toppled from the basket and rolled off the path to nestle in the fallen leaves. Normally, she would have picked it up and brushed it off to eat regardless, but something told her to leave it and she pressed on, not daring to look back again.

After a few hours of walking, the path widened into a small glade. Tacey stopped, wary of stepping into the golden spears of sunlight that pierced the opening in the canopy. Bright green grass covered the ground, reaching towards the light and caressed by a breeze that didn't reach the trees. The path had not been kind to her feet; the ground here looked softer, and it was the only way to go without leaving the path, yet still she hesitated.

A barking laugh startled her from her paralysis and she jerked her head in its direction. A wolf-man crouched on a rock to the side of the clearing, head tilted to one side. Seeing he had her attention, he jumped down and crossed the glade in a few loping strides. His pelt was darker than that of the guard who'd led her to the forest. His smell reached her before he did, feral and musky. She inhaled sharply and took an unbidden step back as he neared her. This close, she realised he wasn't as tall as the guard, but still taller than anyone she knew. His skin had a deep tan despite the dark of the forest she'd seen so far. He wore the wolf pelt much as the guards had, its head over his own, the fore legs loosely secured on his arms, and the rest hanging free. Unlike the guards, his arms were bare: he wore a leather shirt over his torso, but no other obvious armour. Round his neck, a wolf tooth hung from a leather thong. It was larger than the ones on his face.

"This glade won't hurt you." His voice shared a roughness and cadence with the guard, but wasn't as deep. He seemed younger; the wolf-face made it hard to be sure, but she felt he was nearer her age – or would be, if he were human. What she'd suspected when she'd seen the other guard control the wolf's eyes solidified now: when he grinned, the wolf's upper lip peeled away from his sharp teeth. The wolf skull and pelt was part of them. She froze in terror.

"Ugh," he rolled his amber eyes, "this won't do. *I'm* not the one who's going to eat you. I'm going to do everything in my power to get you to Grandma safely." He reached out a hand, palm up. She saw the calloused palm and dirt around his nails, and looked back at his face. The wolf-part was unreadable, but the eye roll had returned her spark of anger, and that gave her the power to ignore his hand and walk past him.

The sunlight was warm, the ground soft and giving beneath her feet. The gentle breeze brought a freshness to the air, and here she could hear the song of small birds, a twittering she'd missed in the darker forest.

"It's safe here," to Tacey, his tone seemed condescending, "you might as well eat."

She looked around the clearing, not wanting to go to the rocks where she'd first seen him. The only other place to sit was the ground, so she smoothed the cape beneath her, careful not to dislodge it from her shoulders as she sat. She placed the basket in front of her and pulled out a small plaited loaf. She held it and thought of her parents and the love they would have poured in as they made this for her, her favourite bread when she was a child. She was not going to cry in front of her guide, but it was hard to hold back the tears. She looked around for him, and saw him to the side, standing with his arms folded and watching her.

"Do you eat?"

The fur above his eye moved as though he were raising an eyebrow and his inhuman mouth twisted mockingly. "I eat."

She leant the basket in his direction, but he didn't react to her implied invitation so she turned it back to her and took an apple to go with the bread. As she ate, she felt a little bit of her start to relax, and realised how hungry and thirsty she actually was. It became easier to eat more, washed down with swigs of cold water. Her guide watched in silence.

Her needs sated, the fear, anger and sorrow were easier to ignore. She looked up at the wolf man. "What's your name?"

He tilted his head again, enhancing his inhuman appearance, "Thunder."

She waited for him to ask hers, or say anything further, but after a silence that seemed to last several minutes she stood up and faced him squarely. "Fine then, *Thunder*, which way next?"

A strange thought crept upon her, and she wondered how much time she had to reach Grandma.

Thunder unfolded his arms and pointed. She walked towards the path he indicated, resolutely not looking at him further. He paused to bury the remains of her meal, then walked behind her, thoughtful.

Tacey was not the first he'd guided, though he was still new to the role. It sat uncomfortably in him, to be leading someone, even a human, to their death. He understood the stakes, maybe better than most wolfsouled, but it still seemed distasteful. No hunt, no test of skill. And on the other side, to choose one of your own…

Once, towns and villages had tried to offer the dying and elderly, but Grandma had demanded younger meat. A child was not big enough to satisfy her hunger, so the duty fell to the young adults. Each town would create a shortlist of those who were deemed to contribute the least to their neighbourhood, and the Sacrifice would be Chosen from these by raffle. Tacey was unmarried and had never settled on an individual role, never rising to make her mark in any field. She was capable, but largely uninterested and easily distracted. She'd hoped the work she did to help her family, especially in helping raise her niblings and her youngest siblings, would have saved her, but it clearly wasn't enough. She tried not to dwell on that, but the knot of anger at being seen as less useful, less *important* started to twitch as she walked. Thunder's appearance of aloof disdain didn't help.

This path was easier going than the first, bumpier but softer on her feet. Even the air seemed clearer. She ate another apple as they walked. She could sense Thunder behind her, but he didn't try to engage with her until she went to throw the core into the trees; he caught her wrist and took it from her with a barked "No!"

She glared at him, feeling like a scolded child. He didn't elaborate, but tipped his head back and awkwardly swallowed the core. She looked away in disgust, and started walking again.

They came across another clearing, much like the first. She stopped again to eat, and again he stood over her until finally she snapped, "Sit, for pity's sake!" and, startled, he did, crouching near her. She saw his gaze on her basket of food, and made a bigger show of pushing it in his direction. His eyes widened as he looked at her again: he was leading her to his death, but she was willing to share her food. Tentatively, he reached out and took a bun. They held eye contact as he reached up to his wolf jaw, and pulled it up and above to reveal a human face. Tacey masked her gasp as he squeezed and stretched his face muscles, warming them up. His eyes opened, and they were still amber filling the eye like a wolf's, and slightly too close together. She looked at the eyes on his wolf skull, and saw with relief that they had closed.

"It's easier to eat this sort of food this way." His voice was different, less resonant. He started to eat, holding the bun before him and bringing his head down to it. Finished, he looked up at Tacey, "I suppose I should ask your name."

That aloofness again. She thought she'd cracked it: she was afraid and needed a friend and this was the closest she had and he can't even be kind. The injustice rose up in her and turned her voice to a whip. "Tacey."

He flinched at her anger, and whispered hoarsely, "My mother's name meant Silence too." He absently caressed the fang hanging from his neck.

Neither spoke again as they finished eating, Tacey wrapped in anger and Thunder in sadness. Again, he buried the crumbs of their meal. Done, Thunder pulled his wolf head back down, opening the eyes again. His ears swivelled and he sniffed the air, acclimating back into the different sensations. He stood and looked down to Tacey. "We should keep moving. There's a good rest spot ahead."

She sighed. Every step took her closer to her death, but she still managed to find the strength to stand and follow him.

The path from this clearing was narrow and strewn with obstacles. Thunder held back brambles and low hanging branches and helped her keep her balance over the uneven ground, and by the time they found the spot he had in mind, she was too exhausted to complain that he expected her to sleep in a tree. Instead, she accepted his help up and settled herself into the nook he'd indicated. The howling started as her eyes closed, distant and dream-like. She thought she was imagining it to begin with, but more voices joined in, getting nearer until there was one beneath her. She looked down, and a dark grey wolf sat beneath the tree, its head lifted to the sky as it joined in the melody. The nights she'd heard it from her home, it had given her shivers of fear that sent her hiding under the covers. Here, the sound was beautiful, and mournful. It ended in a lingering harmony. Thunder climbed up shortly after, wolf and man again, and curled up beside her, back to back. She feigned sleep, and felt his shoulders quiver as though he wept silently.

Morning came. They ate cake in the tree; the magic and the protections on her during this journey extending to the food, which remained as fresh as when she'd entered the forest. Neither spoke of the night before, but both felt a reluctance to move on.

They walked, a smoother path again so Tacey led the way leaving Thunder with his thoughts. The previous Sacrifices he'd led had been very different. Most were scared little rabbits, but one had been a fervent believer in The Cause and so willing, eager even, to sacrifice himself Thunder had felt no qualms about leading him. He'd spoken about how important his role was, and seemed to be proud to have been Chosen. Another had been utterly biddable, apparently unaware of where she was going and to what fate. He'd felt guilty then, but not as strongly as he did now. Tacey understood. Tacey's anger bubbled under the surface and pushed him away every time he tried to approach. Her anger was surely driven by fear, but he wondered whether she, like he, felt an injustice, a sense of readiness to face down Grandma and refuse her fate.

He thought again about how Grandma had torn his mother apart in front of the pack when a Sacrifice she was meant to guide had never made it into the forest. It filled him with fear-tinged sorrow, but he stared at the back of Tacey's head and felt her anger running into him. He chose to welcome it in, rather than to defend himself from it. It no longer felt like a barrier between them, but a bond, and she seemed to sense something to, as she turned to look back at him with an odd look on her face. She frowned, and went back to marching on. Behind her, quietly, he started to sing.

When Grandma is hungry,
Then Grandma must eat,
And the thing she likes best
Is fresh human meat.

Grandma is deadly,
She's fierce and she's strong.
Her eyes are all-seeing,
Her teeth sharp and long.

If you have been chosen,
You mustn't dare run.
Her vengeance is swift:
She'll take everyone.

But her life's not forever,
Death comes to us all.

137

Sound will bring Silence;
With Silence she'll fall.

When Grandma is hungry,
Then Grandma must eat.
And the thing she likes best
Is fresh human meat.

The song never felt as smooth in his mixed throat as in his wolf form, but it still raised the hairs on the back of Tacey's neck. The tune was faster than the song of the night before, more urgent. As he finished, she looked back and slowed her pace so they were side by side.

"I've never heard that sung before," the words were a rhyme she knew well from her childhood, a playground chant that had always spooked her.

Thunder shrugged. "There's a place up ahead, you can stop and get some flowers. Grandma especially likes the red ones."

Again, Tacey had thought they were sharing something and then felt as though Thunder put a wall between them. She sped up to get ahead of him again, hitching the cape awkwardly as she strode along, the half-empty basket bumping against her thigh. Thunder felt her anger bounce against him once more; he wasn't sure how to balance the anger, between pushing them apart and giving them a chance to test his hope. The anger seemed to blanket her from the awful growls, though, or perhaps they were simply beyond her hearing. He knew he needed to handle it, though.

The woodland opened, giant trees standing alone in grassland rather than crowded together as they had been. The path remained clear before them, and passed by a stream that remained lined with trees. One side of the path in sunlight and grass, the other cool and shaded. Shrubs and flowers grew both sides. Thunder waved an arm at them.

"Here. Pick what you want. Wait here. I'll be back soon."

"Fine." *Whatever.*

Thunder tilted his head, studying her for a moment, before pulling the snout of his wolf's head further down and smoothing the forelegs of the wolf pelt over his arms. They merged in, his lower jaw grew to meet the upper fully as he dropped to all fours and ran off as a wolf.

Tacey let out an exasperated sigh, leaning into her anger to protect her from fear. She went to look at the flowers. Pretty enough, soft petalled and sweet scented and beautiful shades of crimson and scarlet and burgundy. Why would she want to pick flowers for someone who wanted to eat her, just because that person liked them? It made her feel sick. She turned her back on the sunny glade and looked at stream. The air felt fresher above the water, the coolness helping cool her anger. She looked to the sky as she felt tears start to fall: tears of anger and sorrow and justified self-pity. She didn't sob, but stood straight and let the tears fall silently. At some point, she realised she was relaxing fists she hadn't realised were clenched. Eventually, her tears ended and she could look around again.

Growing on the other bank of the stream were a few green plants, leaves like arrowheads and tall stems holding clusters of red berries. Her eyes widened as she recognised the poisonous lords and ladies, and suddenly she had a plan. It might not kill Grandma, but she had no intention of being a pleasant meal.

She still had self-preservation despite the journey she was on, and even if she didn't want to make it for herself, thoughts of her friends and family, of the faces and places she loved, pushed her onwards, and that made accessing the flowers harder. She didn't feel safe taking the cape off: it marked her as the Sacrifice, granting her protections from whatever lurked in the forest. It seemed safe enough here, but she'd heard snufflings and gruntings the whole journey, and they seemed to be getting louder and yowlier. The cape was a big drawback here, though: the stream was wider than she could jump, and flowing fast enough that, although not especially deep, she worried the cape would draw the water up to pull her down and away. She studied the trees, but didn't feel she'd be able to climb across without the cape tangling and trapping her.

There were large stones, though, and she was able to manoeuvre them to the stream's edge. She splashed the first in, satisfaction spreading on her face as it settled into place. She nodded and slipped off her shoes, steeling herself to pick up the next stone. The first wobbled a little as she stepped onto it, but she soon had her balance and dropped the next. Seven stones, and she could cross with nothing more threatening than damp feet. A novel sense of freedom settled on her as she collected as many heads of lords and ladies as she dared, carrying them back in the hood of her cape. Freedom, and a sense of power she'd never felt before.

She dried her feet on the cape, put her shoes back on, and picked some other flowers to hide the berries among, in case Thunder saw them and made her throw them away. There wasn't much food left in the basket, so she wrapped what was left in the cloth covering and stashed the flowers beside it.

Meanwhile, Thunder had raced off with barely a glance back. He didn't want to leave her for long, but knew it was a safe place. He headed off ahead, then looped back to chase down the creature that was stalking them.

It was doughy, vaguely humanoid in shape, and had just passed the tree they'd spent the night. The scent trails suggested it had lost them here, and only recently rediscovered the path: it reassured him that the magics on the tree remained strong. He leapt on it, hoping to attack before it was aware of his presence, but it tilted its blocky head and twisted to ram a solid arm into his side. He let out a whimpering yelp as he was thrown to the side. The creature kept walking.

He scampered to his feet and tried again, staying low this time. He went for the back of its legs, and this time got a good bite in before it kicked him with the other foot, and again he went flying. It turned away again, so he chased it down again, getting a good bite on an arm before it swept him to the side once more.

He had its attention; it stood its ground and seemed to be assessing him. He charged at it, aware of its speed and strength now, and ducked under its arm to sink his fangs into its torso. He ripped into it and dodged back, ducking down and back up in time to grab the end of its arm, pulling back and twisting until it came free. He worked on the leg on that side next. It was clearly weakening now, and didn't take much longer for him to rip it apart, scattering crumbs for the birds to feast on.

He howled to his family.

Tacey was sitting at the edge of the path when he got back to her, finishing an apple. She went to pitch the core again, and he realised he hadn't told her why that scared him. Didn't seem worth it, now; they were nearly at Grandma's house, and he'd dealt with the creature that grew from the roll she'd dropped. He caught the core and ate it as before. Tacey watched with that same look of disgust as the previous time, but he could see something else tied in with the fear and the anger, something like... smugness.

Thunder glanced at the basket, and Tacey stiffened slightly in case he saw, but he his only obvious response was "so you found some flowers. Let's get moving." He turned away and started down the path. Tacey glared at his back, but pushed herself to her feet and followed.

"How much further?" They'd walked about half an hour from the stream. Thunder stopped so abruptly she nearly walked into him. He turned, slowly, and she realised she could read his wolf man face, and it was lined with sorrow. His amber eyes blinked, and his hand reached for that tooth around his neck.

"Not far now."

The fear tumbled down onto Tacey. Thunder caught her as she started to implode, a hand on her arm. He pulled her into him, an awkward embrace that became warmer as she sunk into him.

"Don't let the fear hold you, Tacey. The fear isn't you." He hoped he was right. "Find that anger again."

She stiffened against him, pushed back and looked up. "Easy for you to say. You're not the one about to die."

"Ha, there it is!"

She scowled, but something clicked inside.

"I have a plan. I can't promise it'll save you, but maybe it will stop this."

"I'm listening," still wary.

"The prophecy. The rhyme," he clarified at her confused face, "my mum… she said we can't assume it will just happen, we need to push, to *make* it happen."

"Ok."

"It didn't work for her. She never got a chance. But, I think she's right, and I think this is our chance." He'd put both his hands on her shoulders and held her gaze with frantic intensity. She didn't pull away, and one hand went to stroke the poisonous bundle in her basket.

Do I trust him? Is this a trap?

He let go of her to pull the tooth from around his neck. "You'll need to let her swallow you. Are you ready to hear this?" He didn't give her time to reply, didn't dare break the pace of his speech. "She'll swallow you whole. And then, then use this. Stab it in wherever you can. I'll come in, I'll try, but I can't. I'll try to save you.

She took the tooth, cool and firm in her hands. Her thumb brushed the tip, revelling in its sharpness. *Yes, I trust him.* She looked up from it, past the sharp teeth in his mouth, and to those amber eyes. "I had an idea to." Dropping the tooth into one hand, she lifted the posy so he could see the lords and ladies.

He pulled his lips away from his teeth in that grimacing smile. "Here, we'll break them up." He helped her press them into the flowers, hiding them amongst the petals. She wrapped the strap holding the tooth around her hand and hid the tooth in her fist as she practised holding the posy to best hide their tricks.

"Will this work?"

"I don't know, but we have to try." He pulled his wolf-face up so he could smile with a fully human face. She responded better to this and smiled back. Her anger felt strong now, productive and motivating.

They walked on side by side, brushing arms and shoulders. Thunder's wolf-face remained tilted back, his human face exposed to the sun. Tacey looked up at him, stroked her hand over the back of his and started to play with his fingers. He didn't look down, but she recognised it wasn't aloofness or disinterest. His fingers pressed into hers. She was afraid to be eaten, but that wasn't behind the butterflies in her stomach now. And she trusted him to try and save her.

The path led through another small woodland, dappled sunlight cutting through the trees and small birds and animals frolicking. Tacey raised an eyebrow. Thunder put an arm around her shoulder, pulled his wolf-face back. "Nearly there."

He let her go before they stepped into the glade. A picket fence marked off a neat garden, filled with red flowers that surrounded a neat cottage. No turning back. Thunder opened the gate, and Tacey walked through. Neither spoke. She didn't look behind her, but Thunder watched until she had entered the cottage, then pulled his face down fully to wolf, and howled a song.

The cottage door opened smoothly. Tacey chose to walk in with her head high; she was not going to show her fear. The basket remained over her arm, the hood over her head, and the wolf fang wrapped in her hand. It smelt of cut wood and freshly made tea. Large windows let in more light than she was used to experiencing indoors.

A reedy voice called out from upstairs. "Ah, child, you made it!"

Tacey closed her eyes, and started up the stairs. The voice continued, "I'm here, my darling. Sorry I can't come out."

Tacey followed the voice. Grandma lay in a large bed. At first glance, she looked like an elderly woman, but as Tacey looked closer she saw stark differences: the large eyes were red rimmed, the ears came to a point that showed through the wispy hair.

"It really is me; you've made it." Grandma chuckled under Tacey's scrutiny, revealing rows of sharp, shark-like teeth. A cloying sweetness filled the room, like dying roses. Tacey put down the basket and pulled out the posy of red flowers. "Did you pick those for me?" Tacey nodded. "How thoughtful! Now, come closer. I'm soo huungry." Her mouth opened wider as she spoke, snapping at the air. Tacey froze, and the figure on the bed sighed and rolled its eyes. "Come to me. I do not want to have to get up." Her tone was firm now.

Even with a plan in place, Tacey had to force herself forward. Grandma leant forward, sniffing and snapping, her jaw distending further and further as Tacey got closer. Fear swirled around, but Tacey pressed her thumb against the side of the cool wolf's fang to maintain the kernel of anger that powered her.

The jaws stretched, the creature stretched up and above her to dive its head down and swallow her from above without leaving the bed.

Dark, warm, agony.

Tacey struggled, but managed to bring the crushed berries against the flesh pressing into her. It took a desperate eternity, but the *squeeze* of being swallowed paused; the throat spasmed and jerked around her and she felt a spark of hope. The air was getting hard to breathe; she let the posy fall and twisted the fang in her grip. It felt larger, stronger, and she pushed the point against the encasing flesh, pressed it with all her focus, lit it with the anger inside.

Darkness.

Outside, a handful of wolfsouled had responded to Thunder's call. They hung beyond the fence, restless, waiting for a signal. Their sharp ears picked up the gulp as Grandma swallowed Tacey; Thunder let out a little whine as his stomach clenched, and his eldest sister licked his ear.

They waited. They couldn't defeat Grandma unless Tacey was able to weaken her, and they weren't prepared to risk the pack unless they were she had done so. Others had challenged her in the past, and had been destroyed even more thoroughly than the human settlements – only their songs remained.

So they waited, until a thwacking thud brought them to attention. Each wolf head spun to the door, and Thunder led the way as they streamed through the gate, into the house and up the stairs. The largest wolfsouled paused at the gate, shrugged into from wolf to wolf man and grabbed up the axe at the wood pile he'd cut for the beast the day before.

The creature that was Grandma lay in a contorted, distorted heap on the floor, clawing at its elongated, distended throat. Scratch marks showed that the struggle was weakening. Tacey's body bulged within, and Thunder brought his attention to this point. He could see the point of his mother's fang cutting through. The great white wolf man swung the axe and sliced through the neck below Tacey as Thunder shifted into wolf man and reached in to pull her free.

She took desperate, gasping breaths and scrabbled around her, wild eyed. Thunder pulled her close to him, checking her over with anxious whimpers. With his support, Tacey gradually relaxed and looked around her at the strange wolves around her. She recognised the golden eyes of the wolf man holding the axe, and nodded her thanks. Her relief, though, was in the arms of Thunder around her.

They found the strength to stand. Tacey handed back his mother's fang, and Thunder placed it round her neck, and like that they stood and held each other.

It would be a long walk home, but no one else would have to follow her path.

Probably a changeling, **Fern KL Goodliffe** studied maths and drama at university and went on to make little use of that, drifting between careers. She currently divides her energy between teaching aerial circus, being a parent, and writing.

Rival Stars

by Andrei-Ion Ghircoiaş

Esafius never expected the day to come like this. He foresaw a downpour, with only the smell of rain wafting in the air. Bouts of lightning would reveal the sky's unsettling gloom. And the thunders would roar with a might that would put giants to shame, followed by the shriek of a chill wind that would attempt to freeze hope in his veins. But instead of a terrifying storm, this final day came with a bright warm sun casting its comforting light upon a bustling city. Deafening thunders were replaced by spirited conversations or children playing in the wide or narrow streets. And instead of the scent of rain, Esafius' nostrils were filled by the pleasant aroma of fresh cinnamon buns, resting on a silver plate upon the round table of the room.

Everything was unexpected. But then again, so was the letter. He thought at first it had been an uninspired ruse, but something in those words made him reconsider. The tone was different. She did not try to mock, tease or taunt him. It was as if it had been written by a completely different person. But the promise of finality, of seeing their almost eternal dance of death reach its conclusion, spurred on him to come here.

Esafius strapped his turquoise brigandine in silence. He then checked the armor of his arms and legs, and noticed his hands were shaking. His heart was close to a flutter. He took deep breaths, but it did not seem to abate. The conclusion of his mission had been postponed so often he almost forgot it could ever end. And now, after so many years, it came. A delayed inevitability that felt foreign. But for this he had a remedy. He tilted his head back, eyes closed, and placed both hands over his heart. He fell into a deep prayer, asking his goddess to give him the strength to see this through.

And her response did not tarry.

A sudden warmth washed over him, and he felt his worries melt into nothingness. He felt pulled into a tight and loving embrace, like that of a mother given to her child to remind him he is not alone. That someone is there who loves and protects him no matter the circumstances. His hands, almost with a mind of their own, rose and responded to the hug. To an observer, it would appear as if Esafius was hugging the warm air. But in truth, his hands felt a presence there. His shaking stopped, and his heart resumed its normal pace. Then, the embrace ended gently. The goddess was with him. He could not fail.

With a renewed sense of confidence, Esafius donned the golden coat over his armor and went down towards the first floor of the tavern. There were few patrons enjoying their meals and drinks at the tables. A calm before the storm of drunken merriment and joyful music which was a frequent occurrence during the nights. Upon seeing him, the tavern keeper placed both hands over his heart and bowed his head in reverence. Esafius responded by offering him and his establishment a short, but sincere, blessing before stepping outside into the warm breeze of the day.

Men and women roamed the streets, almost all with a sword by their hips. The city of Vidza was known for the fiercely independent spirit of its citizens, and their devotion to the goddess Umphiona.

"Mommy, look! It's the Ferryman!"

Esafius turned to see a small boy pointing at him, eyes wide in wonder, whilst his mother flashed an embarrassed smile. As soon as the boy's words left his mouth, the people nearby paused their conversation or shopping for various baubles and stared. And when they realized it wasn't merely the imagination of a child, the word "Ferryman" spread with disbelief and enthusiasm faster than a fire in a dry forest. They gathered around him, forming a crowd at a respectable distance. Questions were thrown, asking, begging almost, if the goddess was pleased with them. If they had done anything that might earn her ire, and various other concerns of a more personal nature. Esafius felt humbled by their joy and belief in him. To them he was akin to a demi-god, and to an extent one might say it was true. But, despite his pleasure of leading a crowd in prayer and easing their worries with kind words, his mind was only on the letter. Without uttering a single word, Esafius placed both hands on his chest and bowed his head, eyes closed. Their voices lowered quickly, and soon only the sound of steady breathing came from the gathered crowd. Esafius silently begged his goddess to keep them safe and guide them on their paths, and when he felt a sudden warmth rushing through his body, he knew she was listening. When he opened his eyes, he saw the gathered throng was all in the same stance as him, but they soon opened their eyes as they heard the clanking of the hidden plates of his brigandine. The crowd parted, but followed obediently, their whispers barely discernible from the shouting of merchants peddling their wares.

His destination was merely a couple streets away from the tavern, in a home that was almost indistinguishable from the rest. Another house of stone flanked by many others. The windows had their curtains drawn as if the sunlight posed harm to those within. His eyes shifted towards the door and Esafius quickly realized it was ever-so-slightly ajar. For how long? He could only guess. He approached it quietly, trying not to give his presence away to anyone inside, despite the murmurs of the crowd turning to full-blown conversations. He examined it from top to bottom to see if there was even a hint of a trap, but couldn't find any. Satisfied, he unsheathed his arming sword and parrying dagger.

The crowd turned silent as an explosion of sound came from Esafius kicking the door off one of its hinges. A fragrant, feminine, perfume slowly wafted outside.

He charged inside, looking to use whatever element of surprise he hoped he had. In his peripheral vision he saw two assailants, both armed and somewhat armored. He rushed the one on the right, knowing that against multiple opponents his best chance was to be aggressive and quickly cut down the weakest. He knocked the man's mace to aside and followed with a precise thrust into his neck. Esafius' left armed flashed upwards just in time to block the blow from the other attacker. With the fight now equal, Esafius twisted the parrying dagger, pushing the opponent's blade downwards and with the same thrusting motion he dropped his other enemy to the floor. It was over soon. But then his whole body jolted as his ears picked up a burst of rhythmic noise coming from behind. Turning swiftly, both weapons raised in a defensive stance, Esafius saw the crowd applauding as if they were at the end of a moving theatrical play. He shook his head and turned his gaze back towards the interior of the room.

It was marbled in black and purple, the colors touching and mixing together like two otherworldly lovers who understood each other perfectly. Her colors. It was only then that he realized the perfume he had felt earlier was hers. She was definitely here, and she most certainly had more surprises in store for him. And as if to confirm his thoughts, he heard the unmistakable clanking of metal coming from the only corridor of the room.

She was slightly shorter and slender than him, wearing a black brigandine with a bascinet helmet protecting the head and obscuring the face. The white motif in the shape of a clover on her armor signaled that she was a lone mercenary.

Looking to test her skill, Esafius threw a fierce swing towards the helmet, which she almost immediately intercepted and locked into her parrying dagger, pushing his sword away to break his defense. She then followed with a thrust aimed towards the exposed face of his coif, but Esafius was prepared for it. His left arm rose, the dagger meeting her blade, and at the same time he twisted his body so that her sword stabbed the air. Then, channeling most of his strength, he struck her with his left elbow across the side of the helmet. She almost staggered into the wall, but regained her composure and stance quickly. Just in time to raise both her blades to block Esafius' own. And even that effort was almost not enough. Seeing his dagger flashing menacingly towards her, she rolled away, putting again a reasonable distance between them.

Using her natural agility, she began harrying him, her blows managing to nick the calves and less armored parts of his arms. In response, Esafius struck the source of light hanging from above, thus bathing the room in almost complete darkness, save for the sunlight coming through the door. But, he placed himself to block as much of it as possible. As such, the woman lifted her visor.

Esafius slightly lowered his blades in amazement.

Her beauty was simply enthralling. A young ebony visage, of little above 25 years, with eyes that shone like bright amber jewels. She could dazzle many an artist, and stir envy into the hearts of their muses. Seeing his stunned expression, she lunged at him with full fury, but her sword found purchase only in the marbled wall as Esafius pushed it aside at the last moment. He followed with two pommel strikes to her midsection, and then kicked her legs as she stumbled backwards. Before she even realized what had happened, the tip of a dagger was hovering above her forehead.

"Yield." His voice low and cold.

She winced as she felt the pain reverberating through her upper side, but offered no reply.

"Yield!" he repeated, and pressed the tip on her forehead, dangerously close to drawing a drop of blood.

"You ought to finish me off." Her raspy voice felt like fragrant honey. "No one will hire a mercenary that failed in her task."

"Perhaps," he admitted. "But there is no need to venture forth in the same shoes."

She gave a mirthless chuckle.

"And settle for less? Once you taste fine delicacies you don't go back to gruel."

But his reply surprised her.

"Settle for better." He then got off her and extended his hand. "You are skilled and young. You have the years to learn from failure. The Order of Umphiona can offer you that which the path of the mercenary lacks, stability."

She looked at his hand then back at him trying to discern if it was a trick. Through the corner of her eye she could see the crowd was watching with bated breath. She accepted his hand with a sigh.

"I appreciate it, but I must refuse. Despite my failure, the contract I have with her stands. I am to kill you." She tightened her fists as if to emphasize her point.

The crowd could see what looked like admiration shining in the Ferryman's eyes.

"Very well," he said, taking everyone aback. "If Yella manages to escape once more, then, upon my return, we shall fight to the death. But if instead I succeed, you shall join the Order. Are we in agreement, mercenary?"

"It's Visha, and..." She bit her lip as she pondered his proposition. Esafius could tell she was debating if her own principles were satisfied by his promise. "We are in agreement."

With a nod that signaled both the matter and the conversation settled, Esafius stepped through the narrow corridor. This time, as he moved deeper and deeper into the darkness, with only her distinct perfume serving as an invisible companion, no one else followed. The path seemed to stretch all the way towards the bowls of the void, until he suddenly stepped into a spacious chamber. Impossibly spacious for the architecture of the house, but not for the limitless applications of magic. It was well lit, without any visible source of light. The soft fur carpet changed colors at regular intervals. And the rectangle-shaped marble table was filled almost to the brim with delicacies, the smell of spiced meats and freshly cooked side dishes marrying into the air to produce a delight for the nostrils.

At the end of the table sat a slender woman, wearing an alluring and long evening dress in the shade of night, with streaks of purple moving on it as if having a mind of their own. Her raven hair was close to touching her ashen skin. Esafius could tell Yella had changed since he had last seen her, and not for the better. The whites of her eyes had turned black with few spots of ivory in them, yet her irises still shone with the same shade of dark pink. But what was most striking was the black spot on one of her cheeks, showing a red line in the middle which pulsed like a vein.

"Didn't your mother teach you it is rude to keep a lady waiting?" she teased with her characteristic impish grin.

"Yes, but she also taught me to steer clear of certain women."

His dry response made her chuckle.

"Yet here you are. Shows that you have good taste in them."

Esafius approached the table and scanned the room, his eyes resting on the left wall where a huge blank canvas laid.

"Your letter was surprising in both content and urgency."

"You questioned whether I had sent it," she grinned, guessing his thoughts. "I made sure the kiss at the end would dispel any doubts. Did you like it? I chose the lipstick specifically for you."

Esafius ignored her last remark and glared.

"Why am I here, Yella? You said this would be the grand finale so let's make it so. Enough with this charade," he said, gesturing towards the delicacies.

Yella let out a disappointed sigh.

"I almost forgot how boorish you can be sometimes." Her gaze rose to meet his. "When a woman invites you into her abode, and welcomes you with such a lavish feast, you ought to do her the courtesy of thanking her for the effort by at least sitting down and enjoying the meal. It's a bit of foreplay. You should know, you are quite good at it." She ended with a wink.

"So you can try to poison me again?" he growled.

Yella rolled her eyes.

"Please, I am not unimaginative, and you are not that stupid. Now sit."

Esafius gave another quick look over just to be sure that he did not miss any magical trap, and sat down. It was indeed a feast. Meals carefully and lovingly cooked close to perfection, making it almost impossible to decide with which to start. As he reached out for the bottle of wine, wondering why he was playing along, he heard a loud "ahem". He looked to see Yella smirking whilst shaking her empty goblet at him. Without a word, Esafius got up and poured her wine before getting back to his seat. Once more his eyes moved to the black spot on her cheek. He noticed the red line grew bigger for a moment before reverting to its original state. He also caught her subtle wince as it did.

"I would prefer you gaze into my eyes," she huffed.

"How did you get that wound?" he asked, ignoring her comment.

Yella sighed with the frustration of someone having to explain the obvious.

"I was hoping you would be able to draw your own conclusions. I am dying, Esafius. This will be our final encounter."

"Dying?" His eyes went wide. After so many years entwined in a seemingly endless duel, he couldn't even imagine it would end in such a fashion.

"You are sweet," she chuckled. "Unfortunately for myself, I do not have a goddess that can extend my life on a whim. So, I had to resort to various concoctions. And now they are demanding their tribute."

"How long?"

Yella shrugged, visibly disinterested.

"A few hours? A day? Regardless, not long. I've used all of my abilities to postpone the inevitable till you were here."

Esafius felt the words leave him. There was a mixture of emotions swirling within him. On one hand he was glad everything was nearing towards the end. On the other, her words brought him sorrow. But then, he heard a strange noise. It was the sound of rain pouring on something like paper. He turned towards the source and saw that where once was a blank canvas, color was beginning to appear out of nowhere. The many shades married to quickly form a beautiful painting that was almost indistinguishable from reality. It depicted a throne room where a knight in turquoise-colored armor and golden cape was using a shield to block what looked like dark tendrils sprouting from the hands of a regal-looking woman.

"Our first encounter," she smiled, but then her face twisted into a sneer, "and the day your Faith shattered my kingdom and everything I'd built. The day I swore I would see you all buried!"

Esafius wanted to say something, but she slammed her palms on the table, sending some of the plates and glasses for a brief flight.

"No! I am done hearing your false reasons! The truth is I wasn't worse than the other rulers, but better. The people had full belies and entertainment to keep them happy. But my 'sin' was refusing to be crowned by you," she growled. "How dare I, a simple queen, deny the almighty Ferryman?"

He glared, clenching his fists.

"You created a dangerous precedent. Before you, kings accepted the anointment, and with a strong Faith they were far less inclined to wage war against one another. But after your act of rebellion, others joined. You struck a blow against us with consequences that echo even today."

"Good!" she scowled. "I am glad to have struck against a goddess that was happy to send her army of fanatics against me!"

Esafius' knuckles whitened, but despite his rage, something tugged at his heart. Perhaps it was the circumstances of her dying, or he no longer had the will to raise his walls of lies. Regardless, he gave way to honesty.

"She wasn't."

Yella stopped just as she was about to take another sip from her goblet.

"She was saddened by the loss of life. And knowing my actions made her feel this way fanned the flames of my hatred towards you. As if you carried the full blame. The truth, Yella, is that I could have handled your defiance towards the faith better, but I let my ego best me."

She remained silent, looking at him as if she was unsure if this was a dream.

"But what you did afterwards..." Esafius shook his head. "The tortures, burnings, hangings, the destruction, and mayhem you caused after your defeat, all of it is inexcusable."

Yella waved her hand dismissively and turned her gaze to the painting.

"Let's change the subject. I am done having this conversation again."

Then came the same sound of pouring water, and again the colors began to swirl. They entwined, replacing the previous image with that of a meadow at midnight. Where a young woman, with hair of gold and eyes like the purest blue sapphires, rested against the only tree, caressing the cheek of a man who had his head on her lap. A set of turquoise armor sat next to the trunk. Seeing this old memory made him temporarily forget the hatred he had for the former queen.

Yella smiled triumphantly.

"That was the day I almost won. I came close to breaking you like any woman could with a man, by shattering his heart."

Esafius remembered those days. How he fell for that woman, without realizing who she truly was.

"Indeed, but you made a mistake. You fell in love as well."

Again she waived her hand as if to brush off an invisible fly.

"Don't flatter yourself," she huffed, but it was unconvincing. "I merely stopped because it was too easy to break you. I wanted to make you suffer more."

Esafius looked at the painting and wanted to chastise himself. To go back to that day and slap or punch the sense back into his younger self. How easy things would have been had he stayed away. But, somewhere deep inside him, he knew that were he to actually have this chance, he wouldn't take it.

"Still, I can't believe you fell for that trick," she went on. "A stunning young and innocent-looking beauty, who fell in love with you at first sight and wanted nothing more than to hold you and hear your heart speak. You men are so easy to seduce."

His reply took her by surprise.

"Because I wanted to believe it was real. I wanted someone to be there for me. Someone to love me not for my station, but for who I was without the symbols of authority or strength. I wanted a woman to hold, and feel her melt in my arms. I wanted a lover to make me forget about the world for a few hours just like I did for her." He paused, turning and catching a brief warm smile on her visage. "You offered me all these and more. Perhaps it wasn't real in the beginning. But it certainly become so by the end."

"You fulfilled my need," he continued, "so much so that when I learned the truth of who you were, I was only furious. Not devastated."

Yella turned her gaze to the goblet. There was a tense pause where no one uttered a sound, and the plates of food remained untouched. But then, she let out a sigh that sounded like the beginning of a confession.

"When I saw the real you..." she began, starring at the canvas. "The sadness in those eyes, something in me snapped. Here I was, with the very symbol of masculinity resting his head on my lap. The one men sought to emulate. His neck exposed for my dagger to slice with ease. But all I could do was comfort you."

Esafius waited for her to continue.

"In those moments, the hatred I felt for you was replaced by something else." She paused, her knuckles whitening as she gripped her goblet. "And I wanted to maintain the illusion of the young blue-eyed woman, for your sake, forever."

She then leaned back in her chair and pinched the bridge of her nose.

"I must be truly touched in the head..."

Esafius chuckled.

"You women are so easy to seduce with honesty."

"Yes," she admitted. "Yes, we are."

There was another short pause. A welcome respite after the effort of confessing.

"But it didn't last."

She offered a faint nod.

"No." Her tone revealed more disappointment than she would have liked. "I couldn't move past how you destroyed my dream."

"And I how you almost decimated my religion."

It was as if they wanted to apologize to one another, but something prevented them from doing so. And then a familiar sound came again, signaling the painting's change once more. And it kept changing from time to time, revealing past memories both shared. The majority showed the disastrous effects of their duels. The damage and lives lost as they, seemingly eternally, pursued one another. But some brought soft chuckles or smiles, as these were the few moments they sparred with words, in bed, without clothes. And fewer still could make most men blush with the vivid display of their bodies meeting. These last two types, where they somehow managed to temporarily put aside their hatred for another, had the most vivid details. And then, the canvas went back to its pristine white.

She suddenly turned to him, placing her chin on her hands.

"How long have we been doing this, Esafius?"

His reply did not tarry.

"136 years, 8 months, and 12 days." There were also 18 hours, but he thought it best to leave those aside.

Her jaw dropped for a moment.

"My word! Darling, you definitely need a better hobby." Despite her teasing, Esafius noticed appreciation in her voice.

"Are you saying you are not entertaining enough to be my sole hobby?" he smirked.

"Tease!" Her lips curled into a grin as she leaned back into her chair. Her gaze then shifted towards the contents of the goblet.

"136 years," she said after a while, almost in disbelief. "For 136 years you kept your oath to see me dead, and I to destroy you." Her gaze shifted back to him. "Was it worth it?"

He didn't mention that she wasn't the first one who had asked. But unlike the first, this time he had a clear answer.

"Yes, yes it was."

"But you could have had a better life. You could have had children and watch them grow."

"I had." His words took her aback. "And buried them. I wish that fate upon no one."

It took her a few moments before she replied, and in that time Esafius saw the same comforting gaze she had offered him under the illusory guise of the blonde woman.

"So how can you say it was worth it?"

He shrugged as he got up.

"I don't know, but I feel that is my truth. I presume, were I to search more deeply, I would find you as the reason. Strange as that may be."

There was a faint smile on her lips as she watched him fill her glass again.

"I wonder how our child would have looked like," she mused and then chuckled. "With my beauty and intellect, and your infuriating stubbornness, he would have conquered the world."

"He? Why not a girl?"

"Because I always wanted a son." Esafius noticed her eyes glistened as tears began to form. She then took a sip of the wine and placed the goblet back on the table.

"But enough of this," she said, extending her hand towards him with the impish smile back on her face, as if nothing had happened. "I have one last thing I wish to show you."

Esafius rolled his eyes.

"You do realize times have changed, yes?" he replied, helping her up.

"Quite," she laughed, placing both hands on his chest, "and I do believe I had a role to play in that. But I am grateful chivalry is not dead." She ended with a wink.

She slipped an arm around his own and guided him towards the back where once was a bare wall, but now a door stood in its center. Past it, they found themselves upon a balcony overlooking a field of green with only a tree in sight. It was midnight, and the sky was brightened by stars. The depths of her magical talents never failed to amaze him.

"When I was little," she began, looking at the sky. "My mother told me a star was the soul of an exceptional person. Thus, each night I tried to count them." She squeezed his arm as her eyes were welling up again. "And after she died, I could swear there was another star among the others. Do you reckon our souls will be up there too?"

"I... don't know."

She turned her gaze towards him.

"Or, perhaps, you will be up there, whilst I receive my comeuppance in a place of punishment?"

The malice within wanted him to lie. To have this final, vile, victory. But he banished it to the darkest pits of his mind in an instant.

"There is no place of punishment. When we die, the goddess sends our souls towards peace and eternal happiness."

She let out a sigh of relief, as if a crushing weight had been lifted from her shoulders, but winced as the wound increased once more. It wasn't as brief as last time.

"But don't you feel it is unfair?"

"It is," he admitted, looking into her eyes. "But I am grateful it is not up to me to decide."

She nodded just as a shooting start streaked through the sky. She closed her eyes, and for the few seconds she did, seeing her like this, without masks or facades, with her honest vulnerability worn with pride, he wrapped his arms around her. She did not protest or resist, choosing instead to melt into his embrace, and press her cheek on his chest. For that brief moment the world disappeared. Time disappeared. And the worries of today and tomorrow, the regrets of yesterday, all disappeared.

"I wish we had met under better circumstances," she finally spoke, her voice soft as silk.

His lips briefly curled into a poignant smile she could not see, before kissing her hair.

"And now it will never happen."

"It wouldn't have happened anyway," she said, slowly breaking the embrace and placing one of his hands on her cheek. As they stood like this, eyes locked as if having formed an invisible bridge, the queen and Ferryman were gone. In their stead stood two souls, bound together by choice. A choice born from hatred and rage. And, despite how it transformed, it never forgot its roots. "I just wanted you to know how I felt. The truth is, I loved hating you, but I also loved more than that about you."

"As have I."

They stood in tranquil silence, with Yella resting her head on his shoulder. Suddenly, she gasped as the wound increased again. Her legs began to shake and she almost fell over, but he was there to hold her until the pain subsided. Esafius noticed her lower lip was trembling.

"Will you stay with me until the end?" Her pride was unable to hide the small cracks in her voice.

"Of course."

Andrei-Ion Ghircoiaș - I realized from a young age that I have a calling towards writing. My parents supported me every step of the way, and it is thanks to them that I came across guides on how to write, such as Stephen King's "On Writing". And their feedback encouraged me to hone my craft constantly.

Secrets of the Scarlet Sanctum

by Frank Sawielijew

L ike a leather-winged wyvern, Thassa's vine-entangled starship circled above the mysterious red citadel whose spires reached above the jungle's canopy. Its secrets were hers to unlock; she had staked her claim to this planet long ago. A barren wasteland apart from the swamp-plagued rainforest that stretched across the equator, she had ignored it for the longest time. Her domain spanned a multitude of worlds, and her most recent project required one more accommodating to life.

But now that Baral Suur encroached upon it, this planet required her full attention. His mere presence was a provocation, but his attempt to unlock the citadel was a declaration of war. No other building rose from the surface of this world. It stood alone. To uncover its secrets was a joy she had reserved for a later date, but Baral's intrusion forced her hand.

She landed her ship not far from the citadel, but far enough that the wizard would not witness. Branches snapped, trees fell, and creatures scurried away as the mighty vessel broke through the canopy and touched ground. The vinesnakes unwrapped themselves from its hull and crawled into the jungle to feed; a rare luxury for the space-dwelling beasts.

Thassa shoved a thin-bladed dagger and a long-barreled pistol into her belt, and her stockinged feet into a thick pair of leather boots. Her magic wand was clenched in her fist as she left her ship and set out towards the monolithic citadel.

She walked past her vinesnakes, who were capturing prey with the sticky acidic hairs covering their long sleek bodies. Tiny mammals and giant insects alike were welcome snacks for the starved plant-animal hybrids that had fed only on starlight for over a month.

The ground was wet and marshy. Thick mud sucked at Thassa's boots as she traversed it. Soon, the supple leather was stained a brackish brown and her legs ached from the effort of wading through ankle-deep mud.

Nearer the citadel, the ground became dry. She pointed her wand at her stained boots and muttered an incantation, wiping them clean with a wave of magic. Muddy footprints could give her away, and she intended to enter the wizard's domain unseen.

The wizard had erected a small hovel right next to the scarlet citadel, a tiny shed with oddly leaning walls built from simple mud-bricks. The makeshift building's haphazard construction only made the citadel appear more impressive in comparison. From the stratosphere it had appeared as a small red triangle amidst the green belt of the equatorial jungle, but from the ground it was an imposing giant whose foreboding shape sent shivers down Thassa's spine. Three red walls formed a large triangle, and tall pyramidal towers rose into the sky at its vertices. A massive gate of bronze was set into the wall she faced, colored sickly green by layers of patina. Strange angular shapes were carved into the stone above the gate, abstract gargoyles protecting the entrance with their maddening forms.

Were they guardians, they had failed. A man-sized rent gaped at the foot of the gate. Thassa ducked down, observing. She pointed her wand forward and whispered a spell. A new sense awakened in her body, perceiving the presence of lifeforms around her as colorful spots within her inner eye. The jungle exploded with a multitude of tiny colors racing to and fro; a much larger spot moved about in front of her, colored deep red.

The spell had not been necessary. Baral Suur emerged from the citadel, squeezing himself through the opening he had torn into its massive gate. He was clad in a robe of indigo with a band of red running down its center. The russet brown curls of his beard fell over his chest and moved in the breeze. His left hand was wrapped around his staff, the focus of his arcane powers, while his right held a little item Thassa could not make out from this distance. He studied it with great curiosity.

She ducked down even lower. Her dark green dress blended in well with the surrounding vegetation, but her thighs peeked out between the side-slits of her skirt, displaying the bright purple of her high stockings, and the turquoise band woven into her waist-long black braid displayed another speck of conspicuous color. Enough to be noticeable if the wizard looked her way.

He did not. Baral's eyes were fixed on the tiny object between his fingers; he marched into his makeshift hovel without lifting his eyes from it.

Thassa got up and approached the wizard's lair with careful steps. The ground near the citadel was dry and free of vegetation. The soles of her soft leather boots treaded soundlessly as she crossed it.

167

With her wand held out in front of her, she crossed the threshold into Baral Suur's hovel. He stood at a desk cluttered with arcane apparatuses, rolling the little item he had retrieved from within the citadel between his fingers. It was a small hexagonal tube, each side inscribed with symbols of a long-dead language.

He placed it on the desk and said, "You are not as stealthy as you think, Thassa Lantiyya. I noticed your ship before it landed."

"Baral Suur. You have no place here. This planet's secrets belong to me."

He turned around and showed her a broad smile. "I know. That makes their discovery all the more alluring."

She pointed her wand at the small hexagonal object and cast a spell of pulling. Baral anticipated her move and stepped in the way. Her arcane grasp pulled him forward, close enough to strike his staff at her. It hit her knee and knocked her down.

She grasped his robe and pulled him down with her. Thassa's wand dropped out of her hand, and Baral lost the grip on his staff. They wrestled with bare hands now, punching, clawing, pushing. Like a ball of rage, their limbs intertwined, they rolled across the floor. When they came to rest, Thassa found herself on her back with Baral's fingers wrapped around her wrists. His face was so close to hers that she could feel his breath against her skin. Long strands of his beard tickled her lips. His curled up in a victorious smile.

"This planet's secrets belong to whoever seizes them first, sorceress."

"Not you, then, wizard."

She channeled her magic power through her wrists and shouted an incantation. A surge of electricity shot through her arms and sent a shock through Baral's palms. He withdrew his hands and she rolled away, reaching for her wand. Baral's foot was faster. The wand clattered away, far beyond her fingers' reach.

The glint of cold steel alerted Thassa to the dagger Baral held in his fist, and she quickly drew her own. She jumped to her feet and stabbed at the wizard. Her blade sliced through the billowing sleeves of his robe. His carved a third slit into her side-slit skirt. Nimbly evading each other's strikes, their daggers cut nothing but cloth.

Until Thassa managed to touch her dagger against the soft flesh underneath his arm. One push, and it would glide effortlessly into his heart.

But his was at her throat.

They froze, locked into a standoff. Thassa stared into Baral's eyes. They gleamed with excitement. The upward curve of his lips was visible even underneath his long beard. The blood that coursed through Thassa's veins burned hot. The excitement of battle, the tension of imminent death. An invigorating cocktail.

"Leave my planet, wizard," Thassa demanded, almost in a whisper.

Baral chuckled softly. "Or you shall do what, sorceress?"

She slowly inched her body closer to Baral's, keeping her blade firmly pressed against his flesh. The dagger at her throat drew blood. A shallow scratch, but it spilled crimson nonetheless. When her face was mere inches from the wizard's, she opened her mouth. *Or what, sorceress?* She didn't know. One wrong move, and their murder would be mutual. They were close enough that her shallow breaths stirred the hair of his beard.

She bared her teeth in a wide grin. "Wizard, I shall—"

A loud explosion cut off her words. The earth shook and the walls of Baral's hastily constructed hovel shuddered. Her flesh was driven deeper into his dagger as she tried to keep her balance, coloring the length of its blade bright red.

He withdrew his weapon and returned it to its sheath. Enough to tell her the trick was not his.

"Gods be damned! Who dares intrude upon our intimate rivalry? Our deaths should come by each other's hands, and no-one else's."

Another explosion made the walls shudder and the ceiling crumble. Baral pushed Thassa away with a violent push. She snatched up her fallen wand and aimed it at the wizard, but when a hail of bricks rained down before her eyes, she realized that his shove hadn't been an attack – he had saved her life.

Baral emerged from the cloud of dust with staff in hand. A rivulet of blood trickled down his forehead. "Out, before they bury us alive." He grabbed the hexagonal tube off the table and let it vanish inside a pocket of his voluminous robe before he rushed out of the crumbling building. "And let us make whoever's behind this pay dearly for his actions."

"That he shall, my hated rival." Thassa followed the wizard outside and looked up. A cyclopean vessel floated in the stratosphere, its wide belly caressed by clouds. Like blankets of wool they wrapped their white tendrils around the steel colossus. She saw the flash of cannonfire and threw herself to the ground with a curse on her lips. Moments later, explosive shells hit the earth around her. Mud and dust and shards of rock were launched into the air. A hastily cast protective spell shielded her from the shrapnel.

Baral stood with his staff facing skyward. But at this height, the ship was far out of reach. "Someone you know?" he asked Thassa.

She shook her head. "A new player in our game, whose presence is not at all appreciated. I suggest we carry the fight to him. My ship is nearby."

"Mine is further."

"Then I shall invite you aboard." She gave the wizard a stern look. "But if you touch anything, you die."

"Of course. I would apply the same condition if it were my ship."

Thassa took the lead and Baral followed. Under ordinary circumstances, she would not trust the wizard; but their rivalry was deeply personal and an outsider intruding upon it at its most climactic moment did not sit well with either of them. They would vanquish the attacker together. Then, they could resume their quarrel.

The mysterious spaceship kept pounding the ground with barrage after barrage, but its cannons did not follow the two mages as they disappeared into the jungle. The fire was directed at the scarlet citadel.

This was *her* planet! It was Thassa's right to unlock the citadel's mysteries, and these intruders were taking it from her. Taking it in a much more violent, much more permanent way than Baral had attempted: not by unlocking them first and stealing her joy of discovery, but by pounding them into rubble and rendering them forever unknowable. They would pay dearly for their crime. This she swore to the star-gods.

Her vinesnakes poked their heads out of the murky waters when she approached. Slimy swamp-fish and sleek-furred mammals stuck to the sticky hairs covering their plant-green skin. She barked an order and they quickly scurried back to the ship, wrapping their lengthy bodies around it.

"Vinesnakes?" Baral scoffed. "How inelegant. I did not expect you to make use of such primitive creatures."

"Misbehave and they shall have you for a feast." She opened her ship's door with a wave of her wand. "Unlike you, I appreciate the wonders of nature. Perhaps you would be a better mage if you did not dismiss them so."

"Perhaps." He raised his arm when he stood at the threshold of the ship's entrance. A curious vinesnake sniffed at his finger, regarding him with four shimmering black orbs. When he looked up, his eyes found spots of rust where the vinesnakes clung to the hull. "But I prefer my ship not being slowly digested from the outside."

Thassa marched straight into the control room and turned on the engines, initiating takeoff. The canopy cracked and her vinesnakes snatched a last snack from falling birdnests as the ship rose to the sky. All sensors were focused on the gargantuan ship above. It was ten times larger than hers, a massive leviathan that had to be crewed by hundreds of men.

"I hope your ship has enough firepower to make us a way in."

"I trust my vinesnakes to do what they're best at." She showed him a teasing smile. "You shall see what you're missing out on, wizard."

The attackers did not even notice her approach. Thassa grabbed the flight control stick and prepared herself for evasive maneuvers, but no projectiles came her way. She landed her ship on their hull and whispered a command into her wand. Her vinesnakes heard and got to work.

"Their hull will soon be breached. Let us get ready to board." Thassa opened a cage at the far wall of the control room, and a squirrel-like creature climbed onto her shoulder. She whispered something into its ear, and the squirrel nodded its head. She gave it a nut from a pouch at her belt.

Baral laughed. "Another pet, sorceress? How quaint. I wasn't aware you are using your ship as a zoo."

The squirrel hopped off her shoulder and scrambled towards the control panel, sitting down on a brightly glowing keyboard. She showed it a smile, then turned to Baral and changed it to a scowl. "My pets are better company than you, wizard. I assume you are adequately armed?"

He nodded. "I have my staff and a few sidearms under my robe. Enough to bring death upon our shared enemy."

"Then come and watch as my pets create a breach."

Thassa opened the ship's door with the push of a button. Outside, the vinesnakes were spewing acidic bile unto the enemy ship's hull. It was potent enough to eat through the thick layers of metal within seconds.

She jumped onto the enemy ship and almost lost her balance when another barrage of cannonfire sent a wave of vibrations through its hull. At a barked command, the vinesnakes returned to her ship. She approached the hole their acidic spit had created. A smell of blood and vinegar crawled into her nostrils. It almost made her gag, but she controlled herself; she would never show a sign of weakness, however small, in front of Baral Suur.

"Come on, wizard," she said, fingers wrapped tightly around her wand. "Let us leap into the lion's den."

Thassa jumped into the hole and found herself in a large room whose walls were studded with blinking screens and arrays of buttons. She quickly shouted a magic word and waved her wand to shape a protective field. The swarm of bullets flying towards her was robbed of its kinetic energy as it passed through the field, and the projectiles hit her with the negligible force of thrown pebbles. Barely enough to inflict a bruise.

She dismissed the protective field and drew her pistol. Baral chanted an incantation behind her. When the bullet left her gun's muzzle, it split into many parts, each seeking out a different man. Ten tiny shreds of metal found the hearts of the ship's defenders.

"Good choice of spell." Thassa grinned. She had never expected to perform a feat of teamwork with her hated rival, and yet...

"This is not the command center," Baral noticed. "We disabled one of its limbs, but the ship's heart is elsewhere."

"I share your assessment. Let us push onward, then."

Baral pulled a beaked warhammer from beneath his robe, gripping it with his right hand while his left remained around

173

his staff, and nodded. They stepped through a door into the ship's complex network of hallways and fought their way forward. Their movements were poetry. Two rivals focusing their mutual hatred on brutally efficient teamwork. Thassa's bullets pierced flesh, Baral's hammer broke bones, and each wove spells around the other so naturally as if they were one.

The ship's defenders were no match against the mages, but no fear showed in their dull eyes. Even as they fell by the dozens, they kept throwing themselves at the intruders. Thassa blasted a group of them with a spell, yet not one scream of anguish emerged from their mouths as their flesh tore apart.

"These men disconcert me, wizard. They show not a shred of regard for their own lives."

"I would think them automatons were they not made of flesh," Baral said. "Their eyes are without life, their movements without vigor. Perhaps their master has subjugated their minds with a spell."

"So many?" Thassa shook her head. "I doubt there is a wizard in this universe who could uphold an enchantment of such magnitude. The spell would crack under the pressure of so many minds."

Baral grunted. He did not like agreeing with Thassa, but the sorceress was right. No mage could weave a mind control spell at this scale.

They kept pushing onward until they reached the ship's control room. A hailstorm of bullets greeted the two mages, but a defensive spell cast in unison formed an impenetrable barrier in front of them.

"Drop your weapons and surrender!" Thassa shouted. "More men than I cared to count lie dead behind us. Unless you wish to join them – stand down."

The men ignored her offer of surrender. They dropped their guns only to switch to combat knives and threw themselves at the intruders. Not a word came across their lips, not even a roar as they charged. Thassa holstered her pistol and drew her dagger. The men pushed their bodies through the magic barrier and were met by hammer's beak and dagger's blade.

Their numbers seemed endless. For each man killed, another took his place. Thassa focused on the blade in her hand and the foes in front; everything else became a blur at the edge of perception. The crunch of Baral's hammer connecting with bone, the hum of the ship's computers, the clatter of dropped knives hitting the metal floor – it was the beat that gave rhythm to the combat. She fenced with her enemies until her arm grew tired.

It took her a few moments to realize the fight was over after the last man fell.

Only one remained, seated on a sleek black chair in the center of the room. His deep red jacket was decorated with golden adornments. The ship's commander.

Baral approached him with his staff grasped in both hands. Thassa knew what he intended: after a few spells of compulsion, the commander would give any answer Baral requested.

Thassa chose a more efficient way of procuring information. She approached a computer and attached her wand to a port. The cold data of machines was more reliable than the words of men. A short incantation, and her wand downloaded everything on the ship's hard drives.

Baral touched his staff against the commander's forehead, murmured a magic word, and questioned him. "Why did you come here?"

"To protect the Lady's secrets from prying eyes."

"Who is the Lady?"

"The mistress of life and death. Without her, we would not be."

Baral raised an eyebrow. Was the scarlet citadel an ancient sanctum of a forgotten goddess, these men religious fanatics? Then why would they destroy her temple? "Where can we find her?"

"She resides on the third planet from the Sacred Sun. Her palace is crowned in splendor."

"What is the Sacred Sun and where can we find it?"

"A star that shines with golden light. It is thirty-one point three lightyears away from here, towards the outer edge of the galaxy."

Baral looked at Thassa and showed her a nod. "I have the information we need. Let us return to your ship and pay a little visit to this *Lady*."

Thassa pocketed her wand with a grin and returned the nod. It contained much more information than what Baral had squeezed out of the commander.

The two mages made to leave, but a sudden explosion from within the ship's bowels shook the floor and Thassa lost her balance. She heard a crack when her shoulder met hard metal. A curse escaped her lips.

"What was that?" Baral shouted.

"The ship's self-destruct mechanism. You cannot be allowed to leave with the Lady's secrets."

The floor became slanted as the ship descended groundwards. Thassa slid down the smooth metal floor. The pain in her cracked shoulder broke her concentration. She had to heal it before she could fight against the pull of gravity – but the cacophony of groaning metal and exploding fuel tanks that echoed through every room of the ship made it impossible to focus her thoughts on the wound.

She felt a strong hand close around her shoulder and screamed, but a moment later the pain went away.

"On your feet, sorceress. We need to work together."

"Baral!" She almost said *thank you* to her hated rival, but swallowed it before it passed her lips. An unthinkable utterance. "Yes. Quick – to my ship."

"No time. We won't reach it before impact. Help me build a shield."

Baral's knuckles grasped his staff so tightly they were white as bone. With all his power, he pulled thick sheets of metal out of the ceiling and floor and shaped them into a cocoon around himself and Thassa.

Thassa whispered a single word into her wand before she added her efforts to Baral's plan. She threw a short glance at the ship's commander, thinking for a moment that they should drag him into their protective shell – but discarded the thought when she met his eyes. The man stared blankly ahead. Not the slightest emotion showed on his stoic face.

It wasn't natural for a man to face death like this. She channeled all her power into forging a solid iron shell around herself and tried to forget those soulless eyes. Every single man on this ship shared that look.

Had she not seen that they were made of flesh and blood, she would have thought them artificial.

She pulled one last metal panel towards herself and closed the sphere. Darkness engulfed her. The clang of metal echoed through the tiny chamber as Baral beat his staff against the shell. "This should protect us. Brace yourself for impact, sorceress – this will get rough."

"I am well aware, wizard," she quipped as she sat down and put her hands over her head. "There are few things more dreadful than sharing such tight quarters with you."

***

The tight iron sphere was thrown around like a ball when the ship hit ground. Thassa suffered many scrapes and bruises as her body was tossed to and fro. She flung her arms around Baral, and his arms closed around her. Their bodies shielded each other and softened the blows. She felt his heartbeat against her chest and his breath against the side of her neck. His body was warm, his muscles firm under the fabric of his robe.

A good enough thing to hold onto, for lack of alternatives. A human pillow to soften the impact, nothing more.

When the wildly rolling sphere came to a halt, Baral shouted a magic word and the metal sheets fell apart. Finally, there was light again.

Thassa found herself staring into the wizard's face, their lips only centimeters apart. Her heart pounded heavily – the contempt she felt for this man warmed her blood. The iron sphere had been his idea. He had saved their lives. And she hated to admit it.

"We live. Your sphere saved us, although it could have been a little more comfortable."

Baral stood up with a laugh and straightened his robe. It was frayed and torn in many places. "Your plan was to run back to your ship. We would have died in the hallways before we made it there."

Thassa got to her feet and checked on her own clothes. Her dress was missing a sleeve and the skirt was a mess, but her skin had only suffered a few scrapes. She felt worse than she looked – more from having to admit that the wizard was right than from physical pain.

The ship's command room was a burning ruin. Shards of glass from broken screens littered the floor and exposed wires spat out sparks. Rays of sunlight streamed through gaping holes in walls and ceiling.

Broken glass crunched under her boots as Thassa headed for an exit. She squeezed herself through an opening until she passed through the ship's hull. The ground underfoot was wet and muddy. The ship had landed in a marsh.

With a hand at her brow to shield her eyes from the sun, she scanned the horizon. The scarlet citadel was hard to miss. Huge pillars of smoke emerged from its smoldering ruin. It was just as ruined as the ship that bombarded it.

"The citadel's secrets are buried forever," she lamented. "That Lady the commander mentioned... she owes me answers."

"She owes us both," Baral responded. "Your ship?"

"What do you think? Destroyed in the crash." A lie. Her ship was fine, but he didn't have to know. Now that he had seen hers, she wanted to see his. "Where's yours?"

"Not too far. Ten minutes if we walk swiftly." He pulled a foot out of the soft ground. Mud covered his boot up to the ankle. "Fifteen across this ground."

He set out, and Thassa followed. The marshy ground was a pain to traverse. Their boots sunk into the thick, murky water up to their shins and every step was laborious. They could have used magic to ease the journey, but were too busy watching each other's every move. Thassa expected the wizard to pull a trick on her, and he expected the same. They still had a common enemy, but the immediate threat was dealt with.

Their rivalry was back on.

When Baral plunged his staff into the mud and muttered an incantation, Thassa had to laugh. The wet ground embracing her boots turned solid, and she was stuck. "Ah, wizard! It would not be such a passionate rivalry if you could go one moment without betrayal, would it?"

"Do not blame me, sorceress. Had I not betrayed you first, you would have done so later." He showed her a wide smile. "Besides, this is your planet. Does it not deserve to enjoy your presence a little longer while I seek out our mutual foe and pry away her secrets?"

"Make your attempt, wizard." Her eyes gleamed brightly as she looked into his. "These secrets are mine by right, and I shall have them."

Baral pulled the small hexagonal tube from his robe, the one he had found within the citadel, and twirled it between his fingers. "Unlikely, as I have the key. See you on the third planet from the Sacred Sun, sorceress."

He returned the object to his pockets and left Thassa where she stuck. No matter how hard she tried, she couldn't get pry boots out of the now-solid ground. "Pity about the boots," she muttered as she weaved her wand in a wing-shaped pattern, "but it looks like my journey continues on stockinged feet. Arrogant bastard... he'll be surprised when he finds me already there."

She wiggled her feet out of her boots and rose into the air by the power of her levitation spell. A soft word spoken into her wand signaled Oachkat to approach her position. She rose above the canopy and saw her ship approaching quickly.

Her lips curled up in a smile. Oachkat deserved more than a handful of nuts for that.

**

"Good piloting. I see my precious vinesnakes made it out alive, too. And my dearest rival still thinks my ship went down with the wreck. Name your reward, Oachkat, and you shall have it."

The little squirrel hopped off the control panel and climbed up Thassa's leg. She squealed when his claws dug into her flesh. "Sorry. Didn't want to ouch you, mistress. Why no boots?"

"Lost them. Next time, check if I'm wearing boots *before* you climb up my leg. I'm considering to renege on that offer of reward..."

"Oh no no no! I want a bag of thaccriavons. Please!"

Thassa plugged her wand into her ship's computer with a chuckle. Thaccriavons were exceedingly rare nuts that only grew on a planet populated by deadly fauna. Few explorers dared to brave its dangers, making them a widely sought and expensive treat. "We're heading into the unknown and I might need you to pilot the ship again. If you do as well a job the second time around, I'll get you a bag."

Oachkat danced on her shoulders, his long fluffy tail waving with anticipation. She felt his sharp claws poking into her flesh.

"And I would highly appreciate if you got off my shoulder. My dress is ruined enough as it is. You don't have to shred it any further."

Oachkat apologized and returned to his nest. The squirrel's excitable temperament could be a pain to deal with, but his piloting skills were second to none. A valuable companion – and the only salary he demanded was the occasional treat.

Thassa searched through the downloaded data and tried to locate the coordinates to the Sacred Sun. There were a lot of junk files, but strangely enough not a single private log from any of the crew. Not even the commander kept a personal log. Everything was pure data: atmospheric readings, interstellar travel time, solar coordinates…

And there it was. A G-type main-sequence star exactly thirty-one point three lightyears away from here, towards the edge of the galaxy. She entered the coordinates into the autopilot and headed for orbit. Once she was out of the planet's gravity well, the engines would accelerate beyond lightspeed and head for the mysterious star.

She went to her bedroom and fell onto the mattress with a grin on her face. The wizard still had to determine the star's exact coordinates. She was at least an hour ahead of him.

"Those secrets are mine to unlock, wizard. You'll never beat Thassa Lantiyya at her own game."

***

The ship computer's robotic voice woke Thassa from her sleep. "Designated solar system reached. Approaching third planet from the sun."

She climbed out of bed with a yawn. The journey had taken six hours, all of them spent asleep. Her body felt fresh and well-rested, ready to tackle whatever challenges awaited down planetside.

She placed her stockinged feet on the soft carpet and took a deep breath. No need to rush. Baral Suur was far behind. She could take her time and go it slow. Change into a fresh dress, pick out a new pair of boots…

The computer's voice sounded again. "Sensors detect another ship leaving lightspeed behind us. Scanning… scanning…"

"What?" Thassa rushed out of her bedroom and towards the ship's main computer. A wireframe model of the scanned ship appeared on screen. "Baral! Oh, that clever bastard…"

There was no way he could have figured out the star's coordinates that quickly, with only a single hint to guide his search. He must have locked onto her ship and followed her course. His vessel was a mere hundred kilometers behind her own.

"Damn you, wizard! So much for taking it slow." She switched off the autopilot and took the ship's controls into her own hands. Maybe she could still lose him on the planet.

She approached the rocky orb at high speed. The colors that dominated the planet were grey and orange. Neither the blue of oceans nor the green of vegetation showed on its surface. A barren rock, and unlike the planet of the scarlet citadel, this one didn't even have a small strip of life along the equator.

There had to be something. She magnified the image on the screen and strained her eyes to make out its details.

There! Between two mountains, one grey and one orange, was a tiny lake. A settlement surrounded it. It was dominated by a massive structure of vivid crimson. Its color stood in stark contrast to the more muted tones of the planet's natural rock.

Whatever it was built of, Thassa was sure it didn't originate on this planet.

She slowed her ship when it entered the atmosphere, but not by much. She rapidly approached the settlement with the huge red structure in its center. The nearer it came, the more she realized how massive it truly was. Thick walls enclosed a huge central spire that reached far into the sky. The color reminded her of the scarlet citadel, but the architecture differed radically. Where her planet's structure had been bare and angular, this was defined by elegant curves and lavish decorations.

She landed her ship in a large public square not far from the massive structure. "Oachkat, get on the controls. If I need the ship, I want you to react immediately."

The furry little creature scampered out of his nest and hopped onto the control panel. Thassa rushed towards the door and opened it with a wave of her wand.

Her lips uttered a thousand curses when she saw the wizard's ship touching down right next to hers. Baral emerged with a grin on his bearded face and spread his arms in greeting.

"Sorceress! You have a daredevil flying style, but I have a good autopilot." He glanced down at her stocking-clad feet and touched his staff to the ground. "I see you left your boots behind. You should be careful with your steps, lest you ruin those wonderful stockings."

He murmured a spell, and jagged spikes formed on the rock around Thassa's feet. She held out her wand and locked eyes with him. He held her gaze, and a comfortable tension settled between them. Every time they faced each other, they were willing to fight to the death; there was risk in it, but it felt familiar. Compared to the unknown of this planet's citadel, their rivalry offered comfort.

The wizard's eyes glowed with intensity. She wished to leap at him, face him in close combat, wrap her fingers around his throat and squeeze.

But she didn't. Whatever awaited in the bowels of that massive crimson structure sent a shiver down her spine. She didn't want to face it alone.

"Wizard." She let the word hang in the air for a long moment. "We enter that palace together. Once we have gained possession of its secrets, we can fight over who gets to keep them."

Baral turned to look at the imposing structure. Its lavish exterior hid something sinister within. Even though his long beard hid the expression on his face, Thassa knew he felt it too. There was a sense of unease in the rigid stance of his body.

"Agreed, sorceress. This place is best explored with a companion – and we share an enemy in its occupant. We enter together."

He approached Thassa and touched his staff against her leg. A short incantation sent a tingle crawling through her skin. She felt it in the tips of her toes, her fingers, her scalp.

"Another trick?" she asked.

"A boon to let you cross those spikes without drawing blood." He gripped his staff with both hands and repeated the incantation. "The protection will be of use where we are headed."

Thassa crossed the field of spikes Baral had summoned at her feet. The sharp rock shredded the fabric of her stockings but failed to break skin.

They headed towards the citadel together. The town that surrounded it was a strange place. Its buildings were small and simple, fashioned from the grey and orange rock that covered the planet's surface. Each house was a perfectly rectangular box completely lacking in adornment. Similarly bland and interchangeable were its people. Men and women alike sported close-cropped hair and wore tight-fitting clothes of a dull grey fabric. Everyone's hair was black, everyone's skin pale. Their faces showed no expression as they went about their business. They didn't even notice the two interstellar visitors in their midst.

"Just like the people on the ship," Thassa remarked.

"As if they lacked a soul." Baral grunted, expressing his displeasure. "I don't like this."

Neither did Thassa. These people didn't behave like people. No signs of curiosity, no conversations among friends – only blank stares as they ambled stiffly like automatons.

Only when the two mages reached the threshold of the citadel did the people finally react to their presence. Weapons were drawn and shots were fired. Thassa felt a bullet hitting her in the back. It didn't penetrate her skin, but the impact still hurt.

When she turned to face her assailants, she froze in place. Hundreds poured out from the town's rectangular buildings, some armed with guns, some with melee weapons, some only with kitchen implements. The horde crashed towards the two mages like a wave.

Baral touched his staff against the ground and shouted a magic word. The earth shook, but the tremors barely slowed the horde's approach.

Thassa raised her wand to her lips and whispered a command. Even two powerful wizards could not deal with such a multitude alone. Baral tossed devastating spells into their midst that shattered bones and rent flesh, but not a single yell of pain emerged from the crowd.

Only when Thassa's ship descended at them like a bird of prey and her ravenous vinesnakes swallowed rows of people did the crowd's formation break. The ship rose into the sky, only to swoop back down for another attack run. It passed through the town's wide streets at such low altitude it almost touched the ground.

Baral stared wide-eyed at the spectacle. "And I thought I had a good auto-pilot… I'm impressed, sorceress."

Thassa grinned. "It's not an auto-pilot. Come, let's go while they're distracted."

She crossed the threshold into the citadel; Baral followed close behind. A massive tunnel led them deeper into the building, closer towards the sky-scraping spire at its center. Magical lights were set into the walls at chest level, but the tunnel's high ceiling was so far up the light couldn't reach it. Portals set into the walls led elsewhere within the citadel, but the mages ignored them. They marched straight ahead, confident the one they sought resided in the center.

The citadel was eerily empty. It had enough space to house thousands, yet not a soul confronted them on their way through its halls. Only the echo of their own footsteps disturbed the deathly silence.

"A tomb, perhaps?" Baral mused.

Thassa shook her head but said nothing. The Lady that dwelled here was very much alive. She could feel her presence. The crimson stone underfoot was warm against her bare soles, yet a strange chill crept up her spine and made her shiver.

After a long march through the high-ceilinged tunnel, they emerged into the inner courtyard. Tiny canals of fresh clear water ran between the flagstones of a lavish garden. Blue-leafed plants stretched their limbs toward the sun. Their round, symmetric petals were of the same crimson as the citadel's stones.

The central tower rose into the sky coiled like a serpent, every centimeter of its surface adorned with arcane carvings. Its door stood open.

Thassa looked at Baral. Their eyes met. She had looked into his many times before, seen their mischievous glint, their penetrating stare. But in this moment, she saw something different in them. Something she had never noticed before, but now realized had always been there.

She shook her head and discarded the thought. "Ready, wizard?"

Baral nodded. "To tear the scarlet citadel's secrets from the Lady's grip – and then resume our cherished rivalry, my hated enemy."

Thassa's lip twitched at the comment, but it didn't quite form a smile. Oh, how she wished to resume her game with the wizard, but her mood was darkened by dread. Baral's hands were shaking. The wizard felt it too.

Side by side, with staff and wand gripped tightly in white-knuckled fists, they entered the tower. Inside was an impossibly tall chamber, its ceiling so far up that despite the many tall, narrow windows that allowed the sun to illuminate it fully, it could not be seen from the bottom. Right in the center stood a large throne hewn from pitch-black stone. Upon it sat the Lady, a woman of impeccable beauty and frightening presence. Her skin was pale as alabaster; it gleamed like a shining bright star upon her night-dark throne. The long hair that fell to her waist was deep dark bloody crimson, like the stone of her citadel. She was naked save for the golden ornaments that embraced her limbs.

She rose from her throne and welcomed the intruders. "So you made it to my sanctum. An impressive feat. You have earned my respect, short-lived as it may be. Any last words before I wipe you from existence?"

"You assaulted my planet!" Thassa shouted. "You destroyed what was rightfully mine! We have come for vengeance, and to retrieve the secrets you took from us."

"What was rightfully yours?" The Lady snickered. "Adorable. What you sought is not yours to know, little sorceress. Nor is it yours, wizard. When I sensed your intrusion into the scarlet chamber, I sent my men to rectify an old oversight. When I unraveled that little citadel's mysteries many centuries ago, I left everything as it was – now, its secrets are buried. Only a shred remains, but it, too, shall be out of your grasp."

She pointed a finger at Baral's chest and closed her hand to a fist. The hexagonal tube he found in the crimson citadel was ripped from his pocket and landed in the Lady's outstretched hand.

"You poor fools don't even know what power you almost had in your grasp, do you? This object contains the secrets of life itself. In that citadel, which was ancient even when I was young, I discovered how to create life. How to become a god. I created my own race of man, and they worship me as their goddess." She glared at the two intruders, eyes filled with jealousy. "This is a power I will not share. I alone deserve to be a creator of life, an equal to the star-gods who made us."

She whispered an incantation. Her bangles and bracelets slid off her arms and formed themselves into the shape of a snake. She wrapped one end of this golden serpent around her wrist and snapped it at the intruders like a whip.

The golden rings slapped Thassa across the forearm. It stung, but Baral's protective spell kept them from tearing her skin.

"No blood?" The Lady looked at her with confusion, then smiled. "Ah. How adorable. You think your meager wizardry protects you from my wrath." She moved her left hand in a circular motion and whispered silent words.

The next strike of her whip tore Thassa's skin and drew blood.

"I have lived for a thousand years and mastered magic far beyond your limited intellects. Compared to me you are like ants looking at a man, incapable to grasp the greatness of what they see. You will die like flies."

Baral threw a glance at Thassa. "Together. If we combine our powers, we can match hers."

Thassa nodded. "Together."

The Lady assailed them with her golden whip and spells of mind-flaying power. Even when they combined their forces, Thassa and Baral barely withstood her assault. Her relentless attacks forced them to channel every fiber of their arcane might into defense. And when they finally had the chance to launch an offensive spell of their own, it dissipated before it could touch the Lady's skin.

She grasped the hexagonal tube between two fingers and held it up. "Pitiful fools. To think you imagined yourselves worthy of such knowledge... I shall flay you alive for your hubris."

Thassa closed her eyes and took a deep breath. Even together, she and Baral were no match against the Lady. Unless...

"Wizard," she whispered.

"What?"

She knew a way to tap into the hidden strength at the bottom of their hearts. If a bond was made between two mages, if their hearts were made to beat as one, if their union was formed with passion...

She took Baral by the hand and pulled him towards her. He said nothing as their eyes met. They gleamed like pools of deep clear water. His face was so close to hers, she could feel his breath upon her skin. Baral, her rival. Her hated rival.

She pressed her lips against his and kissed him.

Baral's arms closed around her. The warmth of his embrace banished the chill of dread from her bones. Her blood rushed hot, and the pounding of her heart was like a thundering drum within her chest. They unleashed the full passion of their rivalry into that kiss, the years of burning hate... or had it ever been hate at all?

The Lady's golden whip kept lashing against her body while she drowned in Baral's kiss. She felt her skin break, felt chunks of flesh being torn from her back, but the closeness to her beloved rival was stronger than the pain. Her galloping heart slowed down until it reached the same calm rhythm as Baral's.

Her eyes went open and stared into the wizard's. "Baral Suur."

"Thassa Lantiyya."

When the golden whip descended upon her again, she grabbed it in her hand. It dug into her palm and tore her flesh, but she held it fast. "Let us vanquish our common enemy – together."

Baral picked up the staff he had dropped, and Thassa wrapped her free hand around it. Together they chanted, together they wove their magic, drawing strength from the bottom of their hearts that beat as one.

The Lady stepped back, surprised at the sudden force of their magic. "Impossible! How can you–"

Her chest split open and her heart tore out, flying towards Baral's outstretched hand. The Lady fell to her knees with shock forever frozen on her perfect face, and expired.

"It seems her heart could not match the strength of ours, sorceress."

"Nothing matches the passion of our rivalry, wizard." Thassa approached the fallen Lady. The hexagonal tube was still clutched between her fingers. She picked it up.

"The secrets of life," said Baral, his eyes drawn to the little object. "Shall we fight over their possession, or..."

He left the rest unsaid, but Thassa knew what he implied. The men the Lady had created were soulless husks, a pale imitation of living things.

She rolled the little tube towards him and nodded.

Baral crushed it beneath a booted heel, shattering the last remnant of this cursed knowledge.

"There are other planets under my domain," Thassa said. "Other secrets we can fight over."

"As there are under mine. Places so ancient you would eagerly kill me for the privilege of exploring."

"There are many secrets I would kill you for, beloved rival." Thassa approached him with slow, deliberate steps. Each step that brought them closer spread pleasant warmth through her veins. When she stood before him, she put her shredded right hand against his chest and smiled. "But the ones I most wish to uncover are hidden in here."

"Then we shall explore them." Baral placed his hand on her chest, right above her pounding heart. "Together."

They left the scarlet sanctum of a flawed goddess and returned to their ships. The people of the town had scattered and now stood unmoving in its wide streets, the little life they had gone from their soulless husks.

Thassa joined Baral in his ship and ordered Oachkat to follow. There were secrets to explore on the journey back home.

Deeply-buried secrets whose discovery she had long longed for.

A Russo-German author with Bulgarian roots, **Frank Sawielijew** loves to forge fantastic tales set in strange, imaginative fantasy worlds. He writes in both English and German and had a handful of his short stories appear in various anthologies since 2015. He has also written professionally for the video game industry.

Shadhavar

by J. L. Royce

The dusty ride inland from the port of Muza had been slow, through desolate hills, to this ancient trading town. Gianna (Gianni, when she traveled alone) left her mount with the stable boy.

He stared wide-eyed at the little silver coin she pressed into his grubby palm. "For your service—and silence."

The boy promised that her horse would be brushed and well fed and insisted on bringing her to the innkeeper himself, struggling under the burden of her saddlebags.

"Ah, *Maestro* Gianni!" The pig-eyed proprietor snatched away her bags. "Yes, your colleague is here, he is here, good sir!" He glared at the boy, who ran back to his stable. "I shall take these to your quarters *personally*."

He smirked. "The Arab awaits you in the common room."

Gianna watched him scuttle away. No doubt he would rifle the contents, but nothing of great value, or secrecy, lay within her bags. Her money belt was safe around her waist, her dagger concealed. She turned to consider the inn.

The ground floor was divided between a common room and kitchen, the odors of one pervading the other. The dim hall was full of noise and the smell of the cooking, ale, and human excess. Gianna easily identified the Arab, but tarried at the entrance, watching him.

He had chosen a dim corner with an unobstructed view of the room, his back to the wall. A fragrant wreath of smoke from a long, delicate pipe floated about him. His head was encased in an extravagant *ghabanah* of black cloth wrapped low upon his brow.

Though slight in build compared to the average man, Gianna had learned to affect the swagger and style of one to be reckoned with, from her boots and boiled leather cuirass to the ragged, short cut of her auburn hair. She pushed through the weaving, drunken patrons without apology. As she neared his table, the Arab rose and considered her.

"*Tahiat, sayidi*," Gianna said in her halting Arabic, her voice pitched low.

His full lips quirked in a slight smile, and he replied, "*Buona serata…*" He continued in his more than competent Italian, his voice a hypnotic baritone.

"Perhaps we shall use your native tongue? I am Chady." He made a slight bow. "And you would be the merchant…Gianni?"

"Gianni Abericci." She bowed. "I represent my father's trading house, based in Venice and dealing as far as Cathay for over a century."

His dark eyes crinkled in amusement. "And we have business best discussed in private, yes …*signorina*?"

Gianna's hand slid towards the dagger at her hip. "Yes."

"Your quarters? They're very nice," said Chady.

At her expression, he explained, "I informed the proprietor of this altogether disreputable establishment that I had an honored guest arriving and would require his finest chamber." He chuckled, a low rumble. "However, do not set your expectations too high, *signorina*."

"Could you not…"

"Of course." Chady stood and announced loudly, "After you, good *sir!*"

They wended their way through the boisterous patrons, who fell silent and averted their attention at the imposing man's passing. The innkeeper, however, cast a knowing eye in their direction and chuckled, shaking his head before returning to his chores.

"All good," said Chady. "As I've regularly rebuffed the advances of the scrofulous whores who frequent this den, he takes me for a sodomite." He glanced down at her. "Your appearance will only serve to reinforce his suspicions."

Though pleased that her close-cropped hair and mannish manner had served their purpose, Gianna resented the implication.

***

"I have arranged suitable refreshments." Chady closed the door behind them and gestured. A low table for dining in the Eastern style and an array of floor cushions almost filled the small sitting room overlooking the street. Candles burned in sconces and stands. The table was set for two, with a steaming samovar alongside, the air redolent with its brew. Gianna spied her saddlebags through the door to the sleeping quarters.

"Come, sit," said Chady. "Or…perhaps you would be more comfortable without your armor?"

Gianna swore under her breath as she loosened the chest plate and removed it. Her bound breasts were sore, and she longed to massage them.

"You called me *signorina*. What makes you think I am unmarried?"

Chady smiled. "Rough clothes and a bit of dust from the road are little disguise. Surely no man would allow a beauty like you out of his sight for a day, much less the length of this journey."

He gestured at her boots. "May I assist?"

"I'm fine." Gianna folded her legs and perched upon a cushion.

"Then I shall serve." He ran the hot brew into two fine cups. "I took the liberty of ordering a dinner," he said, offering her tea.

Gianna studied the thin lip of the cup, with its intricate design, and recognized quality Oriental work. At a knock, Chady opened the door and accepted a tray of steaming foods, sending the serving girl away and latching it. He placed the tray between them and sat.

Many items were familiar: skewers of roasted lamb and vegetables; bowls of stew, couscous, and fresh fruit; and a stack of warm flatbread swaddled in a cloth. They shared the feast, gathering the delicacies onto bites of bread and sipping their tea. Gianna remarked upon the different dishes, particularly those spices unfamiliar to her.

"You are acquainted with the foods of the East, I see," said Chady.

"Lacking a son, my father brought me into the enterprise to assist him. I handle accounts and manage the ships, usually from home. I have traveled, though always with him before."

"We are wanderers both, then," said Chady. "I have been across the Middle Sea to Roma, a glory in her decay, but have yet to visit your home."

"You've been to the Far East?"

"Ah. The courts of Cathay, and Hindustan, yes, to secure rare spices from their secret sources."

"Where is your home, then?" Gianna asked, offering more flatbread.

"The desert, I suppose. I grew up a sheik's son, the child of his beloved."

"Not his?"

Chady looked away. "Perhaps a tale for another time. We must delay more pleasant pastimes and speak of business."

Gianna gathered her thoughts. "Although a minor part of our trade, my father has in the past acquired exotic beasts for the royal courts of Europe. The tiger, the ostrich—even a young elephant."

Chady's dark eyes studied her. "And now, you seek the Shadhavar."

"Not for me, you understand, but for the honor of my father. It would be a crowning achievement, to produce such a rare creature from its Arabian fastness."

"And you ask my help in this matter." Chady frowned. "To give some Christian king this rarest of creatures, for his sport."

"Think of the pleasure it would give them—and the prestige to your land—to share its sweet song, heard only in legends."

Gianna smiled encouragement, though her eyes darted to her bags lying in shadow. She thought of her bow, and the leather-wrapped butcher's tools: knives, some serrated and others smooth as a razor; and the bone saw. All a hunter would need…

"More have heard the legends than the song," said Chady. "The Shadhavar is a gentle creature, with a disposition similar to the unicorn, of which it is a distant cousin. Its music draws and captivates the listener, man or beast; and this has led some to claim it uses this glamour to hunt. This is not so; it is a confusion with the *siranis*—"

"You've seen it, then?" asked Gianna. "Heard its song?"

"I daresay I have more experience of the Shadhavar than anyone alive. As to the music…"

"Yes?" she prompted, leaning forward. "Tell me!"

Chady said, "It is the sound of heartbreak—why would anyone wish to hear it?"

197

Guileless, Gianna replied, "Can one know love without heartbreak? To live without one is to die never knowing the other."

Chady sat in silence until Gianna was convinced her negotiations had failed. Then he spread his bejeweled hands wide.

"So be it. Who am I to deny the crowned heads of Christendom the soothing melody of the Shadhavar?"

He considered her. "And what do you offer in return?"

Gianna demurred. "I would not travel with the entire sum for fear it may tempt the wicked, but I have sufficient florins to make a handsome down payment." She reached beneath her shirt and loosened the money belt strapped there, then drew it out and placed it between them.

Chady shook his great head slowly. "One can only buy beauty with beauty, love with love; to do otherwise is…prostitution." His lips quirked.

Her expression must have betrayed Gianna's mistrust; or her hand, sliding to rest on the hilt of her dagger.

Chady murmured, "Perhaps some assurance of my ability to deliver…" He reached behind his head, fingers working at the knot of his headdress. "Evidence of my special relationship with this creature."

He unwound his turban. Curls spilled out, blue-black and lustrous, falling to his shoulders. Chady wound up the cloth and dropped it beside him, then bending forward ran his fingers through his mane, parting it to reveal his secret.

Gianna stared unabashedly. The horn rose stiffly from high on his forehead, arching gracefully just above the sable hair. At its root it was as thick as her forearm, tapering to end at the back of his head. The color was sandy, though the distal third was covered in umber velvet like a youthful stag's rack.

Gianna marveled as he turned his head from side to side. At last, she breathed again and asked, "How?"

"My mother fell under the spell of a Shadhavar kept by her *sheik*. She was his favorite *houri*, and so out of his love for her he kept me."

"But how?"

"It is said that, during pregnancy, a woman's fondest longing will be expressed in her child. Thus, a child may less resemble a husband than a lover—or so it is said." He chuckled. "So, I was her wish; or perhaps the product of some more intimate encounter…"

"Can you make the song?" Gianna whispered.

"I have. On a desert night, beneath the endless stars, I have stood upon a tall scarp and let the wind find its voice through me, lovely and tragic. The beauty of it was such that I could have thrown myself down and died satisfied."

Chady rose, so suddenly and smoothly that Gianna drew back. He came around the table and knelt beside her.

"My price is this: we shall make music together, and you shall surely have your Shadhavar."

His solemn eyes watched her as he waited for Gianna's reply. At last, she nodded.

"Wash your hands, then," he said, "and come stand behind me."

Gianna did as he asked, her heart pounding. The big man's head came just below her flattened breasts. She lightly touched the graceful horn, reminiscent of the gemshorn a shepherd might use.

"You'll find the base is stiff, but the shaft is more flexible, towards the end. Have you any musical training?" Chady asked.

"A bit, with the recorder."

"Five holes line either side: one side for joy, the other for melancholy."

"I can play either? How do I tell them apart?"

"You'll find it impossible to employ one to the exclusion of the other, any more than pleasure comes without pain."

Gianna lay the length in her palm, stroked it, and touched the apertures one by one.

Chady said, "I shall exhale through it, as you cover the holes."

On impulse, Gianna gripped the horn at its base and lifted it, eliciting a gasp from him.

"Did that hurt?" she asked, innocently. Gianna thought of the hunt, of severing the rack from a felled stag; the bone saw, then…

"No; it's simply sensitive." Chady cleared his throat. "Shall we begin?"

Her first attempt was off-key and flatulent, and Chady chuckled good-naturedly, offering her advice on fingering. By trial and error, she found the touch needed to produce musical notes and played a slow, simple tune. She stopped when the tears welled in her eyes.

"I don't think I can do this," Gianna said, sniffling. She gently lay the horn back onto Chady's head.

He reached up and wiped a tear from her cheek. "What was it?"

"A lullaby, from my childhood. I—I saw my mother; I felt her kiss upon my cheek…" Gianna turned away.

Chady stood and followed her. She turned and allowed herself to come into his arms, placing her face on his broad chest.

"You hear what you bring to me," he said, stroking her tousled hair. "Are you a child, a man…or a woman?"

Gianna lifted her face and searched his for a reason to trust him.

Chady waited. The minutes stretched out. Then he sighed. "So, we are through here."

He picked up the cloth from beside his pillow and prepared to cover his head.

Gianna saw it was the price she would pay to achieve her goal.

"No; I have loved men, and other women, too; but never have I felt a love that touched my heart. I would know more of this feeling. But…"

"You are afraid," Chady said. "I will make it easier for you to decide."

"And the position…the fingering was awkward," Gianna said.

"We can do better." He handed her the winding cloth of his turban. "Bring this."

With an oil lamp in hand, Chady led her into the sleeping chamber with its simple wooden bed. Layers of blankets and pillows covered the straw-filled pad. Chady hung the lamp nearby, untied his sash, and pulled his tunic over his head to stand naked before her.

"You must feel safe." Chady climbed atop the bed, half-raised by pillows he piled at the head. "You needn't remove your clothes; though your boots would soil the covers."

Gianna sat next to him and pulled them off. A small knife concealed there clattered to the wooden floor.

"Oh, little falcon," he laughed.

"Any traveler should prepare for the worst," Gianna said. She pulled her saddlebags closer, under the pretense of depositing the knife, and left them open with her butchering tools readily at hand.

Chady stretched out his arms to either bedpost. "And so, you will tie me." He nodded at the black cloth.

Gianna instantly saw her opportunity: subdued thusly, she could take what she wanted of him. None would believe it if he related the nature of her crime, or that a slight woman could overpower such a robust man.

She took the cloth, tested its strength, and leaned over Chady. His scent was exotic but not unpleasant, like a rich spice.

She stretched the length behind him, looped the ends around his wrists and tied them with slack enough to avoid discomfort, then secured the ends to the posts.

Chady flexed, his muscles bulging until the bed creaked. "You have some skill with knots."

"Sea voyages can be boring. I filled my time with learning the seaman's tricks."

He smiled up at her. "Now what happens, happens by your will, and not—"

Gianna placed a hand over his mouth, hard; then softened her grip, her fingers tracing his full lips. "Be silent, until we sing."

She loosened the drawstring of her *sirwal* and pulled them past her hips, acutely aware of the mingled reek of woman and horse. Raising one leg and then the other, she slipped off the trousers and tossed them aside. Next came her tunic, pulled over her head.

Gianna unwound the bindings restraining her breasts and breathed deeply in relief as she caressed them. Chady lay smiling up at her, and she admired him: muscled torso and limbs, flat belly, and uncut manhood rising eagerly.

"Let us make music, then," Gianna murmured, and she straddled his chest.

Her hands cradled the horn at arm's length more naturally. Beneath her, Chady's nostrils flared as his chest expanded and Gianna closed her fingers upon the shaft. She moved with the ebb and flow of his breathing for several cycles, then played.

It wasn't a favorite song, just a simple melody she chose precisely for its lack of emotional weight. It gave her time to understand her instrument, the captive beneath her. With more confidence, she chose a song from court, played an introduction, and then sang in her natural, clear voice:

So sweet never sounded Orpheus's lyre

When he drew to himself the beasts and the birds

To teach them of Love, as a child and a god…

When she finished the ballad, Gianna threw back her head and laughed. She glanced over her shoulder at his stiff member and smiled.

"Who is the seducer, and who the seduced?" She ran her hands up and down the length of his horn.

"Who is the hunter, and who the hunted?" Chady replied.

"I know something of the hunt," Gianna replied. "I had glorious hair, waves of bronze, falling to my waist," She rolled her head over her shoulders. "Men lusted after me like some prize mare. I let myself be shorn to make this trip, to find you. Would you be shorn for me?"

Gianna gripped his horn again, and Chady strained upwards. She knew she should end it now, with the knife and saw and blood, but could not resist another song.

"This song…broke my heart when I was young," Gianna said. And she began, her voice strong but quavering, not from weakness but desire, as her fingers worked Chady's horn. He could no more prevent her from eliciting the heartbreak of longing than he could stop breathing. She watched his lips working as she drew the mellow sounds from him, as sweet and saddening as his seed.

"I was visiting another court. There was a noblewoman there…it was the first time I knew such attentions from a woman, such pleasure."

Gianna could feel his breath, hot and damp, upon her thighs. His lips strained for hers until her longing made the ballad's words catch in her throat, and she settled upon his face.

Her fingers danced upon his horn; his song penetrated her with his tongue, his lips whispering wordless into her intimate depths. Hips rolling with his heaving breaths, her words blurred into a melismatic aria. Gianna gripped the horn and arched, shaking, as the song trailed off into a moan.

Then Chady's hands were free, and reaching beneath her, lifted her easily. He curled into a sitting position, her hands still clutching his horn as he shifted her to where his manhood rose in greeting.

Gianna shuddered, staring into his eyes, as he lowered her slowly. Her dampness grazed him, and for a moment her breath caught, thinking he would take her as a sailor might; then the blind conqueror found her portal and stood waiting for the invitation. With a groan, she overcame Chady's powerful hands and took him in.

They kissed, his beard pungent with her tart lust. Her fingers still slid along his horn, the wordless melody rising as he released her hips to stroke her back, grip her hair, fondle her breasts, be everywhere, consume her.

Chady crushed the breath from her in his embrace and growled, in conquest or surrender, as his thrusts slowed. His big hand slipped between them and found her, fingers plucking until at last she released his horn and forgot all but the pleasure of *la petite mort*.

***

Gianna woke in near darkness. They lay entangled in the ruins of the bed like survivors of some magnificent wreck. The lamp had died, and the candles beyond had guttered. Predawn whispered a promise at the shuttered window, but merely a lover's lie. Next to her, Chady lay in a deep sleep, his breathing slow and regular.

Gianna rose to an elbow, and gently placed her fingers on the orifices of his horn, transforming the soft rhythm of his sleep into a melancholy melody. On impulse she brought her face into his hair and ran her lips along the length, excited by the animal smell of him, lanolin and spice, the evening's pleasure re-opening inside her like a flower at first light. She sat back and licked the lingering flavor of him from her lips.

Shadhavar: here lay her fondest desire.

Gianna released him, and holding her breath, slid from the bed into a squat. She found the chamber pot and relieved herself, aware she should have done it hours ago, should have drained herself of him, protected herself. Pushing the pot aside, she found her bags in the gloom and reached in, blindly fingering the skinning knives, and the saw.

Chady groaned, slow and bestial, and Gianna froze.

"*Habibi*…little falcon…" Her fingers clutched the first handle they found and raised it.

He rolled towards her and stared at the cleaver in her hand. "So, it is time for truth-telling."

Gianna saw only sadness in his dark eyes. "I must return with the horn."

"Why?"

"My father—my father was once clever but has had misfortunes. He needs a powerful friend."

"A prince, deserving of a princely gift."

"Yes."

The Arab sat up with a grunt and waved over the chamber pot. He relieved himself and wiped his hand on the blanket.

"So why bring just a horn," he said, "when you can deliver the wondrous creature that bears it?"

"Not…you."

"No."

Gianna blinked. "You can do this? You would give me a Shadhavar?"

"As I promised." Chady smiled. "I already have."

He beckoned to her. Gianna dropped the cleaver into her bag and rose, and he easily brought her onto his knee. "Stay with me, *habibi*…"

She resisted his tender kiss, at first, but soon relented.

"The Shadhavar seduces, and not just animals and birds." Chady's strong hand slid over her belly and rested there. "This is its nature, which I…have inherited. You may stay in this land, with me, and I shall care for you; and after the child is born—"

"Child?" she whispered.

"—you may decide."

Gianna stared dumbly into his dark eyes. "Decide?"

"Whether you would give up our child—your longing—the Shadhavar—to some prince; or raise it, with me, in freedom. You shall decide."

Lyrics adapted from 'Sì dolce non sonò chol lir' Orfeo', a madrigal by Francesco Landini

J. L. Royce is a published author of science fiction, the macabre, and whatever else strikes him. He lives in the northern reaches of the American Midwest. His work appears in Allegory, Fifth Di, Ghostlight, Love Letters to Poe, Lovecraftiana, Mysterion, parABnormal, Sci Phi, Strange Aeon, Utopia, Wyldblood, etc. He is a member of HWA and GLAHW. Some of his anthologized stories may be found at: www.jlroyce.com

Thank you…

Thank you for taking the time to read our collection. We enjoyed all the stories contained within and hope you found at least a few to enjoy yourself. If you did, we'd be honored if you would leave a review on Amazon, Goodreads, and anywhere else reviews are posted.

You can also subscribe to our email list via our website, Https://www.cloakedpress.com

Follow us on Facebook
http://www.facebook.com/Cloakedpress

Tweet to us https://twitter.com/CloakedPress

We are also on Instagram
http://www.instagram.com/Cloakedpress

If you'd like to check out our other publications, you can find them on our website above. Click the "Check Our Catalog" button on the homepage for more great collections and novels from the Cloaked Press Family.

THE SCI-FI & FANTASY WRITERS' GUILD